I Want My MoMA

I Want My MoMA
Copyright © 2016 by James A. Tweedie

Credits

Page 5, *Demoiselles D'Avignon*, Pablo Picasso, New York Museum of Modern Art, altered image created by James A. Tweedie

Page 121 Reference to *Get Out Of My Life, But First Could You Drive Me and Cheryl To The Mall?: A Parent's Guide to the New Teenager*, Anthony E. Wolf, Farrar, Straus & Giroux, New York, NY 2002 Copyright Anthony E. Wolf, Ph.D. All rights reserved.

Page 154, *Self Portrait*, Rembrandt van Rijn, New York Metropolitan Museum of Art, altered image created by James A. Tweedie

Page 155, *Woman with a Pitcher*, Jan Vermeer, New York Metropolitan Museum of Art, altered image created by James A. Tweedie

Cover Design © by James Tweedie includes detail from *Demoiselles D'Avignon*, Pablo Picasso, New York Museum of Modern Art, altered image created by James A. Tweedie

Printed in USA by Dunecrest Press, Long Beach, WA 98631

LCCN 2016910944
ISBN 978-1-945539-02-2   eBook ISBN 978-1-945539-04-6

I Want My MoMA

A Year in the Life of
Mike Maurison
Private Eye

James A. Tweedie

Dunecrest Press

Table of Contents

Chapter 1	*May*	I Want My MoMA	1
Chapter 2	*June*	Ice Cream	15
Chapter 3	*July*	Hope	35
Chapter 4	*August*	A Date to Remember	53
Chapter 5	*September*	A Night on the Town	73
Chapter 6	*October*	Masks	89
Chapter 7	*November*	Thanksgiving	109
Chapter 8	*December*	More than Chestnuts	135
Chapter 9	*January*	Snow	155
Chapter 10	*February*	A Window in the Door	175
Chapter 11	*March*	More Than Meets the Eye	193
Chapter 12	*April*	Arson and Old Lace	211
Chapter 13	*May*	New Beginnings	231

Chapter 1

I Want My MoMA

May

It was an unremarkable, average, normal, congested, noisy, gray day in Upper East Side Manhattan. I left my office early around 2:00 p.m. and hailed a cab. As a 30-year-old guy I was between girlfriends and as a private investigator I was between cases. In fact, if I was willing to face up to reality I'd have to admit I hadn't had a case in over two weeks and as for the girlfriends let's just say that lately I've had more cases than girls.

I was feeling down and needed a quiet place to do some thinking. Not too quiet, though, and not too alone. I've lived in Manhattan for so long that it just doesn't feel right if there aren't people milling around and the sounds of traffic and the subterranean rumbling of the subway aren't somewhere close by.

I told the hack to take me to the MoMA. Of all the museums in New York, the Museum of Modern Art is the place where I can tune in and drop out without having to push my way past a drunk, an addict, or a bum sticking his empty hand into my face palm up.

Back in January I was given an annual MoMA pass by a client. She said it had belonged to her husband. He was, as she so delicately put it, as dead as a squashed cockroach and didn't need it any more.

Now that she was sitting in jail facing a charge of Murder One it crossed my mind that my former client didn't need *her* pass anymore either. I juggled the thought that maybe I could ask her for it but gave up on the idea since I didn't have anyone to share it with anyway.

I watched the meter tick off the fare noticing it seemed to skip the small change and click straight to the numbers that needed paper or plastic to pay for them. It must have been my lucky day because we somehow managed to pull up in front of the museum's 53rd Street entrance before I had to divest my entire investment portfolio to pay the guy off.

The cabby said something as I walked away. It probably had to do with the fact that I hadn't given him a tip. In Manhattan, you can save a lot of money if you don't tip everyone who thinks they deserve one. Of course it means I have to eat at a different restaurant every night if I want to get any attention from the waiters or waitresses but at least I've found a way to save a few bucks to pay for the food.

Robert is the guy who greets people when they walk through the front door. His security guard uniform was

2

neat and trim as usual, complete with that too-big and too-impressive badge. I can't say we're close but he's probably one of the only friends I have who isn't hanging on a museum wall.

One time I saw him wearing a small button on his lapel that said, "Don't call me Bob." That button was the only evidence I ever saw that indicated Robert might have a sense of humor but then again, I'm not much of a life-of-the-party type myself.

"Good afternoon, Mr. Maurison," he said without showing any indication of life except for the movement of his lips.

For months I've tried to get him to call me, "Mike" but he never has, which is just as well since my name is actually "Nesbitt." Once when I was in third grade one of the other kids thought it would be funny to trim my name down to a more manageable size and decided to call me "Sbitt" which, to third grade boys at least, sounded too much like "spit" to let it go. I've been called Spit ever since. But for my clientele and for people like Robert I prefer, for obvious reasons, to be called Mike.

Today, however, after his usual stoic greeting Robert became animated enough to hand me a small brochure.

"Read it," he said. "Someone's been stealing stuff in the museum."

I had never heard Robert be this long-winded before so I asked, "What have they been stealing? Art?"

"No," he answered, "a purse, a wallet, and a fold-up walker."

That was all he said. It was as if he had used up every word in his vocabulary and needed to hit rewind before he could start again with the next patron.

3

I patted my back pocket just to reassure myself my investment portfolio was still there.

"Thanks for the tip," I said as I sauntered towards the double elevators on the other side of the lobby.

There was a special exhibit of Diego Rivera murals on the second floor, recreating his historic exhibition at the museum back in 1931. Nice, I thought, but I had come to spend time with some old friends on the fifth floor.

The Fifth Floor Gallery is filled with paintings by Seurat, Chagall, Picasso, Dali, Cezanne, Degas and other painters representing impressionism, cubism, surrealism and a lot of other isms that give art historians and museum curators something to talk about at cocktail parties.

I've been hanging around the MoMA since I was a kid and there isn't much I don't know about the paintings that hang in this room on the fifth floor. Each painting has a story to tell, and I am always happy to sit and listen to what it has to say. Sometimes when no one is paying attention, I talk to them, too.

Not that anyone cares, but my mom ran off and left me with my father when I was six years old and my father died the year I finished high school. These fifth floor paintings have been the only friends and family who have stayed faithful to me since those long-ago sad days, and the museum has been my home-away-from-home since even before my father died.

Among them all, my favorite is Picasso's *Les Demoiselles d'Avignon,* a large painting depicting five sprawling women with the most interesting faces in the history of art. I have given each of the women a name:

Mia, Magdalena, Marta, Maria and Mara. And, of course, they all call me "Mike."

For years, I have pretended that Marta, the one in the middle, is my mother, waiting for me to come running into her arms.

When I learned that the dames represented prostitutes from the red-light district on Avignon Street in Barcelona, Spain I began to wonder why my mother would want to spend her life hanging around women like that. I fantasized that maybe she was like a Mother Teresa and had left me behind with my father so she could help save people trapped and suffering in sin.

As the years passed, however, none of the women in the painting ever complained to me, gave any indication they were suffering, cried out that they were being exploited or appeared to think there was anything wrong with any of it. Like me, they were just doing their thing and trying to mind their own business. The one difference was that they were stuck in the painting doing their thing forever while I could get up and leave the museum any time I wanted.

On this particular Manhattan afternoon, however, I was in no hurry to leave. There was no place to go and no one waiting for me that I was aware of so I sat down on the small cushioned bench in front of the painting, closed my eyes and tried to hear whatever it might be trying to tell me.

The voice I heard was a soft and very feminine whisper. I must have drifted off or something because it sounded far away and close-up at the same time, like the sound of a trawler coming through a thick fog.

"Can you talk with me, please?"

This time the words were as clear as the water in a mountain lake.

I opened my eyes and saw the most strangely beautiful women I had ever seen.

She was tall and strongly built. Her face was darkly tanned. Her large eyes were set high, framed by a short, sloping forehead on top and a nose below that was, if such a thing was possible, even more tanned than the rest of what I could see of her. Her mouth was small and her lips were pressed tight together in a sort of quixotic, impish smile. Her long black hair fell limp and thin behind her shoulders and down her back.

"Well?" she asked.

I gestured for her to sit and added, "Do I know you?"

With a sigh, she walked around the bench and sat down next to me facing the opposite wall. I swung my legs around so that the *Demoiselles* were now staring at our backs.

When I'm with another guy I can go for hours without saying a word. A grunt or a nod or maybe at most a "yeah" seems to be sufficient. With ladies, however, words immediately start forming long, impatient lines in the back of my mouth, pushing and shoving to get their way to the front. I tried to hold them in check but a few of them managed to slip out.

6

"Maybe I'll talk with you, and maybe I won't."

The words sounded confident and assertive with a touch of sincerity, a dash of measured aloofness and a hint of the possibility of forming a collaborative partnership with or without a sliding fee. I doubt if she saw it that way but at least the ball was back in her court and I could take a short breather from having to say anything else for a few seconds.

The seconds ticked along until there were at least ten or twenty of them registered on the meter. Time was flying by as fast as a freight train parked on a siding in Newark.

Out of the corner of my eye, I could see the security guard assigned to the room today. I could tell she was giving us the two-over. Maybe it was time to go somewhere else.

"Okay," I said, "let's talk. You want a cup of coffee?"

"That would be nice," she said.

I gave the guard a small nod as we passed and noticed that she watched us until we disappeared into the small café just outside the gallery.

I ordered my usual house blend black and the girl ordered a "*Batido de Fresas*," a drink I had never even noticed on the menu before. It smelled sweet and looked pink, almost the same shade of pink as her hands. I didn't mean to stare, but I couldn't help but notice the skin color on her hands did not match the skin color on her face. It wasn't even close. It was almost as though there were two completely different people hiding inside the loose-fitting dark slacks and the white ruffled bolero blouse she was wearing. In spite of that, or maybe because of it, I had the strange feeling I had seen her somewhere before, maybe in some sort of public place like an elevator where we might have bumped elbows and said, "Excuse me," to each other. How she knew me, I had no idea.

I started the conversation with, "Have we met before?"

"Yes," she answered in a voice so soft I could hardly hear. "Sort of . . ." she added.

This time, wanting to keep the conversation going, I blurted out, "So, what do you need? A few bucks, a beer, or a back rub?"

She didn't laugh. In fact, her wry smile flattened out and her head sagged. My thick skull allowed the thought that this was probably not the time to engage in small talk or witty repartee.

"What's the deal?" I asked. "What's going on? If you want to talk, I want to listen."

I offered her the wadded up handkerchief I carry next to my cell phone in my left front pocket. She declined the offer but at least the small mysterious smile returned to her face. After taking a deep breath, she began to talk with the same soft whisper, a whisper that was much harder to hear in the clattering café than it had been in the quiet gallery across the hall a few minutes earlier.

"I'm stuck, but that's alright, it's okay," she said as she paused to take a sip from her drink.

So far, *not* so good, I thought to myself. The lady was making as much sense as launching a gravy boat with a bottle of champagne.

She continued, "It's not really about me anyway. There is a woman, and I really like her, but she feels so sad. I've known her for as long as you have been coming to the museum. I wish I could get the two of you together

8

so you could talk, but we've tried, and you've tried, but it just doesn't ever seem to come out the way we would like it to . . . ."

Her voice trailed off, and after another sigh, the seconds began building up on the meter once again.

I am, as I mentioned earlier, a private investigator. I am good at what I do—at least most of the time—but this lady was out of my league. I had listened but failed to understand a word she said.

She raised her head and looked me straight in the eye. For a moment, I thought she was going to finish her sentence, but the moment passed and the seconds started adding up like a CPA during tax season.

"Can we go somewhere else and walk while we talk?" she asked.

"Where do you want to go?"

"I just want to stretch my legs a little. It's been such a long time . . . ."

Her voice trailed off yet again, but this time without a sigh.

"Let's go downstairs," she suggested. "I hear there's a garden there."

"The Sculpture Garden?" I replied. "Sure. Sounds good to me."

We walked to the elevators and went down to the first floor. As we stepped out, we made a quick left turn and entered one of Manhattan's few functional oases. We were greeted by the sound of water and the soothing softness of greenery.

It wasn't long before my newfound companion said, "Oh, what a cute little goat!"

The small bronze statue, almost hidden in the shade, was quietly munching on a small patch of ivy. Her eyes moved from the goat to me.

"I am, as you know, more than a little partial to Picasso."

Actually, I hadn't known that piece of trivia before and as far as I was concerned she still wasn't making a whole lot of sense. After strolling around the pools, we pulled up two chairs and sat down under the expressionless gaze of Aristide Maillol's *The River*.

She spoke first.

"I don't have a lot of time and there is something you need to know."

"Go on. Go ahead. I'm all ears."

"Do you believe that dreams can be real?"

The question caught me off guard and I found myself moving my head in an awkward sort of circle as I tried to shake it "Yes" and "No" at the same time.

"Don't worry about it," she said. "It doesn't really matter because I can assure you that dreams are real whether you think they are or not.

"When you dream you create a reality that over time can sometimes begin to take on a life of its own. It is still your dream, of course, but it can become so real that it begins to speak new words, not of your own imagining, into your heart and scatter the seeds of new dreams, not of your own making, deep into your soul."

I listened, hoping she would get to the point if there turned out to be one.

"When you dream," she continued, "you create new worlds and bring new people into being—people who, apart from you, have no real existence of their own. Yet, like young birds pushed out of their nests, those phantom figures, spawned by your imagination, can take flight and soar into life and love, friendships and adventures, of which you, the dreamer, will never be aware. Often, real people will find their way into your dreams where the dead can be given new life and where the living can be reshaped into whatever you want them to be."

She had talked for a long time and although I had trouble understanding everything she said, it had started to sound as though there was some sense to it. As far as I could tell, she was actually talking the way a sane person might talk if they had something to say about dreams and dreamers. But I was still not sure what this all had to do with me,

"Mike?" she asked. "Or should I call you Nesbitt?"

At the word, "Nesbitt," I felt my body tense and my face redden.

"How do you know my name and what do you mean by, 'Nesbitt?'" I demanded.

I was trying to stay calm but I blurted out the question loudly enough to cause people nearby to turn their heads in our direction.

Nobody had called me "Nesbitt" since my father died, and I couldn't for the life of me think how she could have known it was the name my mother had given me when I was born. I frantically searched my memory, wondering if she might be an old family friend or a distant, long-lost cousin.

"I just want to tell you that your mother loves you very much and is very proud of you."

"My mother?" I stammered.

11

"Yes, your mother," she continued. "Since you dreamed us into existence I have spent my entire life looking straight at her. I hear every silent, secret laugh she lets out when you visit and see every tear she sheds when you leave. I see it all and because I love her I have grown to love you, too."

I stood up.

"But I don't know you," I asserted. "I don't understand. Where is my mother? What are you talking about?"

She kept her eyes fixed on mine and said, "I have made up none of this. Someone else created us but you were the one who breathed life into us. I am grateful to you for all of it. Although I have known you since you were a child, today is the first day I have been able to see you face to face the way your mother does."

I opened my mouth but nothing came out but a long line of question marks.

After a pause she added, "I am not exactly sure what's happening or how, but I assure you that your dreams are more real than you can ever know."

With that, she stood up, kissed me once on each cheek and started walking towards the lobby.

After a slight hesitation, as though she wasn't sure about something, she turned back in my direction and said, "My name is Mia. It is a good name. I am glad we could meet like this today. I will tell your mother everything."

Mia! I wanted to run after her but my feet felt as though some clown had poured cement onto them when I wasn't paying attention. By the time I reached the lobby the doors to her elevator were already closing. I knew where she was going but the only thing I could do was wait for the adjacent elevator doors to open. I rushed in and pushed the button for the Fifth Floor. As I stepped out, I caught a fleeting glimpse of someone with long black hair wearing dark slacks and a white blouse entering the gallery. By the time I got there, she was gone. Except for the guard, I was the only person in the room and I didn't even bother to ask if she had seen anybody walk by.

Instead, I slowly walked over and sat down on the bench in front of the *Demoiselles* from Barcelona.

Mia! I knew I had seen her someplace before.

Mia's smile seemed to grow a little bit larger. I followed her gaze to the center of the painting where I saw, for the first time since I was six years old, my mother as someone who still loved me. I pulled out the wadded up handkerchief from my pocket, wiped off a tear and blew a kiss at one of the most famous nude women in modern art, a woman who just happens to be my mom.

Reality is a hard thing to get a grip on sometimes. One moment you are experiencing it first hand, up close and personal and the next moment you are scratching your head and trying to figure out what just happened. If this story means anything at all, that's got to be it.

I walked to the elevator with a small bounce in my step, pushed the down button and exited at the first floor lobby.

I walked up to Robert and said, "Hey, Bob, when you get off work, do you want to go out and get a beer?"

For a moment, Robert didn't move; but then, as if he was the Tin Man in the *Wizard of Oz* getting a shot of

WD-40 in the neck, he slowly and almost imperceptibly nodded.

And with his lips moving as little as necessary he said, "Sure."

Chapter 2

Ice Cream

June

I have a friend who flew out to Salt Lake City for some sort of a meeting. When he came back, he talked about the clear mountain air. He said the whole thing made him nervous.

I asked him, "Why?" and he said, "I didn't feel comfortable breathing something I couldn't see."

He was glad to get back to Manhattan.

Today was one of those days when the air was thick enough to chew on between meals. On my current budget, breathing is sometimes the only way I can reach my minimum daily requirement of magnesium, iron, and other minerals and heavy metals.

A small desktop oscillating fan on my desk made a soft whirring sound in the hot and humid afternoon. The fan had never moved a breath of air but the gentle hum provided a sort of placebo effect that made my cramped office seem less stuffy than it actually was.

It was 3:15 in the p.m. when I heard a knock on my door. This surprised me for two reasons: The first was that no one had come by to see me in over a week, and second, the street entrance one floor down had a security lock that only opened with the press of buzzer button. Whoever was at my door hadn't been let into the building by me.

This is New York City, and you never know who might be standing behind a closed door. I opened it anyway. My loaded Blue Bersa .380 was in the desk drawer if I needed it and I was desperately in need of a client. Lately, business as usual had been no business at all. There didn't seem to be anyone in Manhattan who had any need of a private detective since Giuliani chased all the resident criminals, thugs, and graffiti artists across the river to Jersey.

I had high hopes the knuckles knocking on my door belonged to a raven-haired, mysterious dame with spike heels, a tight dress and a large, fashionable hat. When I opened the door it turned out to be a dame, but without all the accessories.

Short, streaked blonde hair, an Old Navy sweatshirt, red pajama pants and over-worn green sneakers embraced one of the least stunning thirty-something women I had ever seen.

Without a word, she walked past me to the chair in front of my desk and sat down with her back to me. Without a word, I managed to get back to my own chair without kicking over the wastebasket jammed between the desk and the wall. I sat down and we gave each other the once-over.

After an awkward silence, her voice joined in a sort-of duet with the desk fan.

"A UPS guy had the downstairs door propped open so I just walked in," is what she said. "I hope I didn't break the law or something."

I gave a slight shrug and then a nod as if to say, "Go on, I'm listening."

She took the hint.

"Are you good at this?" she asked. "I mean the private eye thing. You know, if someone paid you to find their baby or something, could you find it?"

I was already getting irritated by the phrase "or something" but her question was a good one and it stumped me. After all, a baby is a hard thing to find once you've lost one. But I needed a few bucks and offered the hint of a smile when I gave my answer:

"Sure. I could find a baby. Been there, done that."

When she didn't respond I added, "What's the deal? Did you lose a baby or something?"

Inside I groaned. The annoying phrase "or something" had apparently decided to move across the desk and into my mouth

"No. Not a baby," she said. "But I did lose something and I want you to find it. I'll pay you whatever your going rate is. I'll give you one hundred dollars as a down payment and you'll get the rest when I get my ice cream machine back."

I felt my tongue tying itself in a knot and I couldn't think of anything to say except to ask, "What did you say? Could you repeat that?"

I was holding out the faint hope she had actually said something besides "ice cream machine."

17

Her reply triggered another interior groan.

"I said I want my ice cream machine back."

She spoke with more emotion than I thought necessary for a small kitchen appliance.

"My boyfriend took it when he dumped me and moved out of my apartment two weeks ago. I was at work, and when I came home, the ice cream machine was gone. I don't want him back, just the ice cream machine. That's all. Here's the hundred bucks. It's yours if you take the case."

I didn't want the case but I did want the c-note.

Against my better judgment I heard myself saying, "Sure thing. It's a deal. Fill me in on the details."

If love of money is the root of all evil, then I had just pawned my white hat for some cheap change. But then again, who needs a hat when you can grab the chance to pay off some back rent.

"Go on," I added. "Why is this ice cream machine so important that you're willing to pay me more than the thing is worth? I don't get it."

"It's from Krup's Kitchen and Bath and I paid good money for it. I want it back."

My tongue began to re-knot itself but I managed to keep a straight face and squeeze out some words that sounded like, "Whatever you say and whatever you want is okay by me. If it's findable, I'll find it."

What I wanted to say was, "This isn't one of those *Candid Camera* deals, is it? Help me out here or you can just forget the whole thing. And please close the downstairs door on your way back to wherever you came from."

But the lady looked so serious that for a fleeting moment I actually felt that finding her ice cream machine might turn out to be the most important thing I would do in my entire life. Fortunately, as I just said, the thought only lasted a moment before vaporizing into oblivion.

I knew the whole thing sounded nuts, but living on peanuts seemed better than dying on a starvation diet so I said, "This seems to be important to you and I guess that means it's important to me. I'll give it my best shot."

She spent the next 15 minutes answering my questions, most of which had to do with the boyfriend. Her description of the ice cream machine was as detailed as it could be without giving me a serial number.

Before she left, she handed me a card with her name, address, and phone number on it. In the corner of the card was a photo of an ice cream cone with three scoops that appeared to be chocolate, vanilla, and strawberry. Her name was Harriet Espy.

I handed her my card that had my address and phone number on it. Across the top were the words, "Mike Maurison. Private Eye." That's it. Nothing fancy. Sort of like me.

As it turned out, the whole case unfolded as easily as a crisp new shirt taken out of a dresser drawer. It cost me five bucks at one of those "find-your-lost-friends-and-relatives" websites, and through some sort of cyber-magic, her ex-boyfriend's address and phone number popped up like a bar of Ivory in the bathtub. I figured he must have had the place for a while—at least longer than the two weeks since he cleared out of Harriet's apartment. It crossed my mind he might have a secret second life and a second girlfriend or a wife on the side. It may have crossed my mind but I didn't really care about the details. All I needed to do was to get the cash-cow ice cream maker back to its owner.

The next morning I took the 66 bus across to the Upper West Side where it conveniently stopped a few blocks from the guy's apartment on West 69th. The street is a shady lane with some pleasant-looking buildings just a few minute's walk from the Lincoln Center. On the sidewalk was one of those "only-in-New-York" signs that always make me feel embarrassed for living in Manhattan: *No Horn Blowing Except for Danger*, it said. After double-checking the address I had written on a junk mail return envelope, I walked up to the door hoping I wouldn't need to blow a horn in the next few minutes.

As I stood looking at the locked door wondering how I was going to get in, Harriet, of all people, gave me an idea. Next to the door was a series of apartment numbers with intercom buttons. The number I was looking for was there but I pushed another number instead. No one answered so I tried another.

On the fourth try a tired voice said, "Who is it? What do you want?"

"UPS," I said.

To my astonishment, the buzzer buzzed and I pushed the door open.

What a putz, I thought to myself.

I walked up to the third floor and stood in the stairwell looking across the hall at the ex-boyfriend's apartment door.

A cell phone call to his number brought a quick answer.

"Yes?" the voice said. "Who is this?"

"Excuse me, but is this apartment 33?" I replied.

"Uh, maybe. It depends on what you want."

"I'm with UPS and I have a package for you down by the street door. If you want it you'll need to come down and sign for it."

There was a short pause and then, "Yeah. Okay. Just hold on. I'll be right down."

A moment later, the door opened and out came the clone of Dustin Hoffman's character "Ratso" from *Midnight Cowboy*. Harriet must have been really desperate to have settled for this guy. To my relief, he took the elevator. I figured I had about three minutes before he came back up, scratching his head and wondering what the heck was going on.

As soon as the elevator closed, I scurried over to his door. He had left it unlocked and I saw myself in. Hoping no one else was home I made a beeline for the kitchen and there it was—the ice cream maker—sitting on the counter. It was exactly as Harriet described it.

I picked it up and almost dropped it. She hadn't told me it weighed 40 pounds. With a slight stagger, I managed to close the apartment door and see myself out by way of the stairs.

"Ratso" was nowhere to be seen, so I hit the sidewalk at a fast pace heading towards Broadway with the loot stashed in a large Macy*s bag I had brought for the occasion. Because it was so heavy I had to cradle it in my arms like a four-year old baby.

When I got back to the bus stop, I put the bag down on the bench and felt pretty good about myself. A poster advertised the Metropolitan Opera production of Berg's *Wozzak*. It crossed my mind that I didn't have enough

21

savings to pay for a standing room ticket. Thank god for that. I can't stand Berg.

In any case, it took less time than the opera's first act to get back to my office. I called Harriet to let her know she could come over and pony up. She didn't answer her phone and she didn't answer it that evening or the next morning, either. At lunchtime, I took the 102 uptown to the address printed on her card.

Property does not come cheap in Manhattan, and vacant lots do not stay vacant very long, at least from the north end of Central Park south. Harriet's address appeared to be an exception. Gravel and weeds behind a Cyclone fence offered a not-so-subtle hint that the lot had been vacant long before Harriet appeared at my office door.

I went back to the office and took a closer look at the ice cream maker.

It wasn't one of those oaken bucket things from my childhood with the metal canister and crank handle that freezes the cream mixture with crushed ice and rock salt. It was a state of the art Lello 4080 Musso Lussino stainless steel wonder. It looked new, as though it had just come out of the box. I plugged it into a wall socket and, although it started humming along with my desk fan the stirring blades inside the removable bowl stood as still as a flamingo ornament on a suburban lawn.

I turned it off, took the bowl out and looked inside. It looked as good as new. Underneath there were some screws holding the thing together. My Swiss Army knife came into play as one-by-one the screws twisted their way onto my desk.

Inside there was room to spare, as if something that should have been there had been removed. In its place was a dark blue velvet bag wrapped in duct tape and held tightly to the inside of the ice cream maker with four twisted wires.

I set the knife on my desk and sat down in my chair. I put my hands behind my head and fell deep into thought. I had a bad feeling about this and my gut-level feelings were rarely wrong. With my guts, if I had lived in ancient Greece I could have been an oracle with temples built in my honor. This time my guts told me the case had taken a very bad late-night u-turn in a very bad neighborhood.

I knew I shouldn't touch the bag but I knew I would. The thought of Greece brought the image of Pandora and her infamous box to mind. What pestilence could possibly be hiding in that velvet bag? Cocaine? Anthrax? A map showing the whereabouts of Jimmy Hoffa? In a moment I could be famous, rich, or dead. I paused for another microsecond, chose Curtain #2 and twisted the four wires loose with the knife's can opener blade.

When it came loose, the bag felt heavy and a little lumpy. It reminded me of the velour bag of marbles I owned when I was a kid—only in miniature. Red marbles and blue ones, cats eyes and agates, large and small, smooth and chipped, I loved them all. They were my treasure. The image of teeny-tiny marbles pouring out of the bag in my hand made me smile. Maybe there was a treasure inside after all.

I cut through the duct tape carefully and loosened the tie-string. Even in the dim light of my dingy office, the diamonds gleamed like stars on a winter night—and there were almost as many of them. Some were small but most were not. I'm not a jeweler, but I once bought a ½-carat engagement ring for a friend who didn't want to go into the jewelry store himself. He said he was afraid he would succumb to the temptation to buy a ring with a diamond so large he would spend the rest of his life bankrupt, in jail, or hiding from creditors. I guessed that most of the stones in the bag were in the two-to three-carat range, along with several that were large enough to be used as functional paperweights.

I had an old-fashioned letter scale rusting away behind the blinds on my window sill. I blew the dust off and set the bag down. I realized I had forgotten to breathe for the past minute or two and let out a heart-felt sigh punctuated by a soft whistle. At the current postal rate it would have cost me nearly four bucks to mail this bundle to Albuquerque—almost exactly eight ounces—a half-pound of cut diamonds—not counting the two large ones that I hadn't even bothered to weigh.

I didn't want to take the time to boot up my computer so I grabbed my trusty 1998 *Information Please Almanac* and flipped to the weight conversion page. Eight ounces of diamonds calculated out to 1,134 carats.

I sat back in my chair and decided to boot up my computer after all. I was so stunned that it hadn't yet occurred to me I might be a dead man sitting. Stealing stolen diamonds is not the best way to make new friends.

The screen on my computer lit up, I logged in, clicked to the Internet, and did a little research on diamonds.

It isn't easy to figure the value of diamonds. The quality of the cut, the size, the color, the weight, all factor in. But it's probably safe to say that one two-carat diamond is generally more valuable than two one-carat diamonds. I didn't want to take the time to add them up one by one, so I did the best I could and took a long-shot guess. The bag of miniature marbles was worth somewhere between five and twelve million dollars.

I had once carried 5000 $1 bills to the bank for a client. They fit into a small shoebox. $5,000 was a lot of money and I was sure I was going to be mugged in broad daylight as I walked down 42nd Street. I tried to imagine what 10 million $1 bills would look like. I figured I would need a small truck but the internet said they would make a stack over 3,500 feet high—the equivalent of three and a half Empire State Buildings standing on top of each other.

I turned off the computer.

The bag of diamonds sat on my desk staring at me. I stared back. Our eyes locked for nearly a minute before I blinked first and turned my head to look out the dirty, street-facing window behind my chair. I would have thought that finding $10 million worth of diamonds would make me feel very happy, but it didn't. Instead I felt numb and cold. My emotions had joined the geese and flown north to the arctic. My guts had been right. Whatever feelings I had were definitely not pleasant ones.

I considered my options.

I could take the diamonds and run but where would I go and what would I do with them? I couldn't just drop one on the counter of a 7-11 to pay for a Slurpee. Besides, Harriet, or whoever she was, could look me up just like I had looked up her boyfriend. No doubt the boyfriend could track me down, too. Stealing diamonds usually means that someone will be cashing in their life insurance.

I could call the FBI and enter a witness protection program for the rest of my life. I could relocate to Nome, Alaska, and go back to using the name my mother had given me, or the nickname I had been stuck with since I was a kid. But the thought of living in the tundra and being called Nesbitt or Spit didn't appeal to me much either.

I could anonymously mail the diamonds to the De Beers' corporate offices on 5th Avenue or, even better, I could for less than four bucks mail them to some randomly-selected sucker in Albuquerque.

I asked my guts for advice but all they did was grumble for having missed out on breakfast and lunch. So instead, I turned to my professional experience for guidance.

"Solve the case," my experience whispered.

"Why should I?" I whispered back.

The conversation was not off to a good start. Sort of like the last three dinner dates I could remember from my dim and distant past.

"Solve the case yourself," came the answer. "You're a private eye for god's sake or at least that's what it says under the name on your office door."

It dawned on me that not one of these options presented itself as a good career move. As a final insult, the last one offered the not-very-attractive opportunity to retain myself as my own client without any money to pay myself for the trouble. *Pro bono*: a charitable donation to the cause of social justice. A nice deduction on my income tax assuming I had any income to be taxed, which at this particular moment in time seemed even less likely than usual.

26

I needed more advice, so I called up my friend Jim Beam from my lower-left desk drawer and spent some time in consultation. Unlike the last time we had gotten together, my head actually cleared up enough to figure out what I needed to do. What I needed to do was to buy some more time and think the whole thing over again from the beginning.

The idea of buying time reminded me of Thor's Coin and Pawn Shop just down the street. I put the bag of marbles in a small cardboard box and wrapped the whole thing tight in two layers of my own duct tape. One medium sized marble found itself taped up inside a small scrap of cellophane left over from a fossilized, half-eaten sandwich I had found lying next to Mr. Beam. The tiny bundle fit nicely into the secret spare key holder in my wallet.

I put the ice cream maker back in the Macy*s bag and carried everything down the stairs and up the block to Thor's.

Thor is the owner and operator of the shop. The first time we met, I was surprised to discover he was neither Scandinavian, Teutonic, god-like, or blonde. The only hammer he owned was a heavy sledge for sale in his front window. Thor, as it turned out, was actually Vietnamese. His English was good, having learned it as a kid back home during the war where he had made his living selling fake Hmong artifacts to unsuspecting GIs. What his real name is I have never found out, but he is proud of the fact he made it in this country without ever driving a cab or working in a convalescent hospital.

He greeted me with his usual question: "Hey, Mike. You gonna redeem your Samurai sword? It's still here, unsold, holding my investment hostage. Don't you miss it yet? One more week and it's all mine, for what it's worth—which isn't very much, as you well know."

"Hey back atcha," I said. "No, you can keep the sword. That's not why I came in. I need a favor."

Thor's friendly smile disappeared in an instant.

"Favor?" he asked. "What sort of favor?"

"Nothing much. I've got this broken ice cream maker and I want you to hold onto it while I find out how much it might cost me to fix it. If I can get it working, I'll make you a deal for it. If not, you can keep it. It's actually quite valuable."

Thor did not look impressed but shrugged his shoulders with a sort of "Sure, why-the-hell-not" look of resignation.

"Oh, and one more thing, could you stash this box in your safe for a few days? Believe me, it's not a bomb or anything like that. I just need to keep it safe for a while before I let go of it. It's sort of a private eye thing."

Thor looked unconvinced.

"Here, let me make you a deal. What's in this box is actually pretty valuable. If I don't come back to claim it in 10 days, it's yours. Think of it as being like one of those "grab bag" gifts you buy sight-unseen at a discount toy store or like one of those oysters that might have a pearl in it."

Thor stuck out his hand and took the small box.

He waved at me to put the Macy*s bag on the counter and said, "You want a receipt for this?"

Thor never really says more than he has to. Even so, he is loquacious compared to my friend Robert over at the MoMA. I didn't have the inclination to say anything else

28

so I just shrugged back at him and walked out of the store.

I hadn't been thinking about the Museum of Modern Art until that moment but it suddenly seemed like a good idea to head over there and have a chat with my mom. The walk took a little over an hour. I stopped to buy a hot sausage from the food cart next to the General Sherman statue before leaving Central Park behind and turning west on 53rd.

My mom doesn't really hang out at the MoMA except in my imagination. But I have a really good imagination and my mom, who is incarnate in the central figure of Picasso's *Les Demoiselles d'Avignon*, is just as real to me as Thor.

My friend Robert was at his usual place at the 53rd Street entrance looking resplendent in his well-brushed security guard uniform.

"Good afternoon, Mr. Maurison," he said with a nod.

Normally I would just say, "Hi, Robert," and leave it at that but today I had a question to ask him.

"Hey, you remember what you told me about the stuff getting stolen around here? You know; the wallet, the purse and the fold-up walker? How did that all turn out?"

Robert paused like a super-computer crunching a boatload of googolplex calculations.

Eventually the whirring stopped, and without a word wasted, he said, "Solved."

"Hang in here with me for a second," I said. "What do you mean, 'Solved?'"

After another, shorter pause, Robert explained that a woman and her two friends hatched up a scheme to steal each other's stuff here at the museum. They were going to

29

establish a pattern of theft and then have an accomplice claim that something of great personal value had been stolen. After that, they were going to sue the MoMA for lack of proper security and collect insurance money.

The length of his reply was as epic as a film by David Lean.

"So," I asked, "what happened next?"

"Nothing."

"Nothing?"

Robert didn't answer but it didn't take a super-computer to figure that the women hadn't been charged because they hadn't done anything illegal—at least not yet. You can't charge people with stealing from themselves and, except for the false theft reports to the museum, the women hadn't actually caused harm to anyone.

I emitted a politically incorrect grunt and went up to the fifth floor to talk with Mom.

Mom stared straight at me with those dark, deep-set eyes as though trying to figure out why I hadn't stopped by to see her in the past three weeks. Unlike my encounter with the bag of marbles I didn't get caught up in a stare-down contest. Instead, I initiated a pre-emptive strike and blinked first just to get it out of the way. Then I got down to business.

When I talk to Mom, I never need to speak out loud or to even think the words. In some ways, it's like the way the Bible says people can talk to God: "When we can't find the words to pray, God fills in the blanks" or something like that. So, I just sat on the bench in the middle of the gallery and let Mom fill in the blanks for me. There were a lot of blanks to be filled in.

To my disappointment, Mom only filled in one of them.

"Robert," she said.

That was it: "Robert."

Somehow I knew she was right. I had no idea what Robert had to do with anything but I had confirmation from two reliable, independent witnesses—my guts and my mom—that he had something to do with something. So I said "Goodbye" to Mom and took the elevator back down to the ground floor.

"Hey, Robert," I asked. "When do you get off work today?"

He looked at his watch as though it was going to give him the answer.

"At closing—5:30. In twenty minutes—Why?"

Out of the clear blue it hit me. Robert evaporated from my mind and all the blanks began to be filled in one after the other like a patient intake questionnaire at the doctor's office. The whole *satori* moment flew by in a blur and then Robert popped back into view.

"Uh, nothing," I stammered, unsure of what I had just asked him.

"Nothing," I repeated. "It's okay. Maybe later. I'll talk to you later. I gotta go. *Ciao.*"

And I left. But this time, I took a cab straight back to Thor.

As usual, I paid the fare but skipped the tip. The sound of a car horn followed me into the pawnshop but I figured it was more likely an expression of anger than it was an exception for danger. Thor's was open until 6:00 p.m. so I got in before the security grill closed off the front door from the sidewalk.

I pulled out my wallet and Thor's eyes opened wide with what turned out to be misplaced hope. Instead of cold cash, I pulled out a small piece of cellophane. I opened it, held the diamond out to Thor and without a word dropped it into his hand.

Thor looked at it and then looked at it again. He pulled out one of those monocular jeweler's magnifiers and looked at it one more time.

"Where did you get this?" he asked.

"Oh, some client gave it to me instead of paying cash for a bit of sleuthing I did for him."

"Well then," Thor said, with the hint of a smile creeping across his face. "You got scammed. The rock is as fake as your Samurai sword."

So, I thought to myself, Mom, my guts and Robert had been on the right track all along.

Like those dames at the MoMA, the whole thing had been a scam—a set-up—and I was the *putz*.

Somewhere out there, probably in that West Side apartment, Harriet and her sleazebag boyfriend were laughing and clinking Champaign glasses as they celebrated some sort of *coup d'etat* of someone's insurance company. Something had been switched and I had been left holding the bag.

At the time I had no idea what had actually happened, but it was all the same to me.

I didn't have to move to Nome, Alaska; I didn't have to be renamed Nesbitt or Spit; I didn't have to enter a witness protection program or be on the lam in fear for my life; I didn't have to spend four bucks on postage; and, as a bonus, I got to keep the hundred dollar retainer.

A semi-sweet end to the case, but that's my favorite type of chocolate anyway.

After 10 days, I figured Thor had probably taken the small velvet bag out of his safe. I have no idea what crossed his mind when he opened it. I didn't ask, and he didn't tell. And as for the ice cream machine, it appeared in his shop window a few days later with a card that read: "Make an offer. Needs work."

I could have taped the card to my office door.

Chapter 3

Hope

July

What does a socially challenged, 30-year-old, single male do in New York City on the Fourth of July? That person is me, Mike Maurison, and I have absolutely no idea.

Macy*s does a spectacular fireworks display at 9 p.m. each year, from barges in the Hudson River from about 71st Street south but unless you know someone with a yacht, pay $160 to watch the show from the *USS Intrepid,* or find a spot to camp out with thousands of people in Riverside Park South before they close the gates for the evening at 4:00 p.m., you're more or less out of luck.

Of course, there are bars where you can go to be with people, watch the fireworks on TV, and oooh and aaah together. I suppose there could be a girl or two to sit with, but the boys usually outnumber the girls by five or six to one, and with those odds, I might as well play the lottery.

As a private eye, I prefer to work solo so I guess I've gotten used to having myself as my best friend.

Another place to go would be Coney Island where they don't usually have fireworks but they do have the annual Nathan's Famous Hot Dog Eating Contest. Forty thousand people turn out each year to watch fools and idiots try to eat as many hot dogs and buns as they can in 10 minutes. The last time I checked, the world's record was around 68 for the men and 41 for the ladies. One dog is usually enough for me, unless I've got a cold beer with time on my hands, and then maybe I'll eat two. If I had cable and cared enough, I'd watch the contest on ESPN later in the afternoon, but I don't so I didn't.

My fridge was empty and my freezer looked the way the inside of the Ice Palace in *Dr. Zhivago* would have looked without the furniture. So I went down to the local market and bought two frozen chicken pot pies for a buck-fifty each.

I came back to my apartment, nuked the pies so the crusts would be as rubbery as possible, turned on the TV, ate the pies, and watched the live broadcast of the fireworks. My chest swelled with pride, and my stomach growled along with the "Stars and Stripes Forever" until I took some antacid to settle it down. I lost consciousness around 10:15 p.m., hoping that July the Fifth would turn out to be one day better than the Fourth.

I can't really say the next day was any better but it turned out to be a lot more interesting. A man came in who had set up an appointment with me a few days earlier. His name was Philip Gorman. He looked my age, but more meek and mild than I am. He looked almost milquetoast-y, like Mr. Peepers, Pee Wee Herman or

Clark Kent. He was not the sort of person I would have expected to show any moxie, but he turned out to be as assertive as Teddy Roosevelt charging up San Juan Hill.

Whatever it was that had stirred him up enough to look me up must have still been fresh on his mind, because he was still hopping mad. When he sat in the folding chair I use for clients, he dropped like an *Acme* anvil landing on the head of a coyote.

"I'll get that guy if it takes all the money I have and every day I have left to live!"

I chalked this up to hyperbolae but it turned out he meant every word of it.

"This is what I want you to do," he commanded, as though he were General Patton addressing the 3rd Army. "I want you to find the guy who hit and ran my brand new BMW at the Quik Park down in the Village. I didn't see the guy hit me but a woman did and gave me a description that matched the video captured on the parking lot's security camera."

I let him finish, and then waited while he came up for air.

"My insurance company is ripping me off to the tune of $5,500 dollars, which is what it is going to cost me to clean up this mess. I'd like to sue them, too, but I'll give that job to my lawyer.

I've heard you're good at finding things so that's why I'm here—to pay you good money to look for the guy and even more if you find him. By the time I'm done he's going to wish his insurance coverage had been in eight figures."

He stopped and glared at me across my desk like he was Fess Parker staring down a bear on the old *Davy Crocket* TV show.

After a few moments I said, "There are nearly two million vehicles in New York City and more than that if you count Jersey and Long Island."

That's all I said. I hoped it would slow him down a little but he was on a roll, heading down a steep hill without any brakes.

"Sure there are a lot of cars," he countered, "but only one of them hit my car. That should make it easy for you. ONE CAR!"

William Blake once said, "To be in a passion you good may do. But no good if a passion is in you." This guy was definitely in the "no good" category but a job is a job and I don't make any dough by saying "No" to a paying customer.

So I said, "I'll take the case but you've got to give me more to go on than that."

"Sure I've got more. I've got plenty—just not enough for me to put it all together by myself. It can't be any harder than finding a dog, right?"

What I didn't tell him was that after looking for two or three dozen dogs in Manhattan over the past six years I've found exactly zero dogs, not counting the ones that wound up at the pound.

"Okay," I said. "What have you got?"

He told me that his parked car had been hit at an angle at the right-rear end, shattering the brake and back-up lights, crumpling the right-rear fender, crushing the rear bumper and popping the trunk open permanently. The vehicle that hit him was described a large, light blue, late model SUV with New York plates. The woman who witnessed the collision didn't see what make or model it was, but the security camera appeared to show either a Chevy Tahoe or a Yukon, two cars, which as I can attest as a world-class expert on automobile rear-ends, are too much alike to tell one from the other, especially on a fuzzy, out of focus, black and white video showing the back end of a distant car moving away from the camera. Hey, I can't even tell the difference between a Tahoe and Yukon from a hundred feet away in broad daylight.

He went on to explain that he would have known the vehicle was light blue even without the woman because a lot of it had scraped off on his white BMW.

"My guess," he added, "is that the SUV also took some of my white paint along as a souvenir."

According to Gorman, there was no way to assess the damage to the SUV, but there was a considerable amount of shattered plastic on the ground that wasn't from his car,

"What did you do with it?" I asked hopefully.

"I guess," he said, "it got swept up and thrown out after the cops took down the report."

I started to say, "You should have kept it as evidence, you numbskull," but I didn't.

Before he left, I got the make, model, and year of his car and the date and time of the accident: 4:30 p.m. on June 15th. This guy had been angry a lot longer than I'd thought.

I told him that the time I would have to spend on the case would probably take a serious bite out of his retirement, but he said, "Just keep it honest and I'll pay whatever it takes."

I had two ways to go with this. I could go through two million car registrations and make a list of all the blue SUVs in the Greater New York area, or I could contact all the auto body shops in a 20-mile radius, on the assumption that whoever hit my client's car would not want to be driving around with a crumpled front end decorated with a dash of white paint.

After calculating that the first choice would take me 15 years, I decided on the second one. A quick look through the relevant Yellow Pages showed there were a lot of auto body shops, but not as many as I had thought. I knew that Thor, the pawn shop owner down the street, had a nephew named Zach who was looking for work. So I talked to Thor, and wound up hiring the nephew and one of his friends to make phone calls and ask questions for me while I made better use of my time.

After two days, Zach and his pal came up with a list of twenty body shops that said they might have done work on a car of that description in the past three weeks. How they couldn't remember something like that, I have no idea, but at least they came through better than the forty-two shops who told the boys to mind their own business, in words that were, no doubt, more flowery than that.

I decided to waste my time on the twenty that offered some possibilities. Speaking to people face-to-face usually pays off better than a phone call, especially when the payoff involves twenty dollars palmed in a handshake. Isn't it funny that, after years of doing business this way, inflation hasn't had much of an effect on the twenty-dollar pay-off? I guess it's because the next bill up is a fifty, and, by consensus, that is too much. It would also be awkward to hand across three tens and a five, or to hand someone a twenty, a one and thirty-five cents change. That, I guess, is why twenty bucks will still buy you a decent table at a restaurant or information from an auto shop. Even so, twenty stops at twenty buck a pop was going to cost my client a significant dip in his quarterly earnings.

After picking up a rental car, I decided to visit the shops in the Bronx first, then Queens and then Brooklyn. Alphabetically, "Bob's A-1 Auto Repair" seemed like as good a place to start as any. When I asked, no one at the shop had any idea who Bob was or if he even existed. So I talked to Ernie instead. I explained to him who I was and what I was up to. He asked me how high the fender had been crumpled, and exactly where the blue paint had come off on the Beamer. I said I had no idea, and he said the information would go a long way in figuring out the make and model of the SUV. I asked if it would have also helped with determining the model year, and he said he already knew it was a 2012.

"How in the world do you know that?" I asked.

"Because, assuming it was a Yukon or a Tahoe, that's been the only year in the last five years that either of them had the option of a light blue color."

I made a mental note to kick myself when I got home for not having thought of that myself. I felt more like a dunce than a detective.

After Ernie said he had never worked on a 2012 Yukon or Tahoe of any color, I said "Good-bye" and "Thanks." I really meant it when I said "Thanks," because I didn't even have to part with a twenty.

"Miracle Body Shop" was next on my list. Manuel wouldn't say much until I gave him a twenty and only then was he willing to tell me he hadn't made repairs on a car like that, either. It took me most of the day to make the rounds of auto shops in the Bronx and Queens.

If I passed a shop that wasn't on my list, I stopped and asked them about the car, too. I talked to a lot of shop owners and found I enjoyed the conversations even when, as it did in every case, I made no progress in my investigation.

I've always thought of myself as sort of a down-to-earth, ordinary guy, but I was surprised when I discovered how smart and knowledgeable some of these shop owners were. The surprise wasn't so much in discovering they were smart, but in discovering that for some reason or other, I had not expected them to be smart—or at least not as smart as they turned out to be. This ego-deflating discovery led me to imagine a new sign on my office door that read, "Mike Maurison, Snob." I made a mental note to kick myself a second time when I got home. In any case, my visit to Brooklyn would have to wait until the next day.

On my way back, I came up with another idea I should have had before I started my tour of the Greater New York area. As soon as I could, I rang up Zach and told him I'd pay extra if he'd phone auto parts stores and ask if anyone had recently purchased a left front light system for a 2012 Yukon or Tahoe. He said he'd get on it in the morning.

That night, I looked through some brochures I had collected on European museums. I have read everything there is to read about these places, and even before I learned how to read, I spent many an afternoon looking at the pictures in books my father had checked out of the library. I knew the National Gallery in London, the Louvre in Paris, the Rijksmuseum in Amsterdam, and the Uffizi in Florence as well as if I had been there in person. I knew where every painting was hung, where every stature was displayed and, even though I couldn't care less, I knew where the ceramics and furniture were, too. I always sleep well when I have something nice to dream about. As usual, the brochures worked better than a sleeping pill.

The next morning, I checked out the shops in Brooklyn. Around Noon, I stopped by Nathan's Famous Hot Dog Stand at Coney Island to see if they had any red-hots left over from the Fourth. They said there was one kicking around in the back of the kitchen somewhere so they sent someone to see if they could find it. If there had been trumpets, they would have brought it out with a full fanfare. Nathan really knows how to make a customer feel like a king or a queen. Since I was working and driving, I had a soda instead of a beer and because I didn't have time to kill, I only had the one dog.

By 2:00 p.m., I had been to all the places on my Brooklyn list, and was not any wiser for it. So I headed home, returned the car, and went down to the MoMA to say "Hi" to Robert and my mom. After my usual promenade around the fifth floor gallery, I made a quick stop on the third floor to see some photographs by Diane Arbus that had recently come out of storage. As usual, her pictures of contorted and distorted circus and freak show performers gave me chills. I needed a reminder that "normal" was just another word for "boring and ordinary." For some reason, the pictures helped ease the stress of another frustrating and fruitless day. Lately, I had felt anything but "normal."

When I was on the subway heading back to the Upper East Side, my phone rang. It was Zach, calling to say that a Napa Auto Parts store in Hoboken had sold a left front headlight assembly to a body shop in Jersey City.

The next morning I took the train from Penn Station to Grove in Jersey City. From there I caught a bus that dropped me off just a block from the car shop. I went inside and spoke to the guy behind the counter.

"Hi, I own a 2012 Chevy Tahoe that took a small hit on the driver's side door. It's nothing, really, but it's driving me nuts because everything else still looks as good as the day I bought it. Have you ever worked on a Tahoe or a Yukon before?"

His answer did not surprise me.

"Yeah, as a matter of fact I did. Just two weeks ago we fixed up a 2012 Tahoe. The left front end needed a lot of work but we fixed it up nice. A small dent in your door shouldn't be a big deal. Bring it in and I'll give you an estimate."

"Sure," I said. "That didn't happen to be Bill Hancock who brought that car in? He's my neighbor down the street and he bought his Tahoe the same week I did. He told me he knew a good auto body place he would recommend to anyone who needed one. I bet this is the place Bill was talking about."

Flattery may not get you everything but it can open doors to places where you can snoop around. He fell for my story like a stuntman in an old Hollywood western.

"Here, let me take a look," he said.

I sidled over a step or two and peeked over his shoulder.

Needless to say, the name that came up on his computer was not Bill Hancock. Even before he told me it wasn't Bill Hancock I was able to see the name "Milford Berringer" and part of an address that said "47-something" and "Brookdale-something." I was on my way to earning a big payday for sure.

After a little more legwork, Berringer checked out to be the bad guy. The auto shop's "before-and-after" pictures showed a streak of white paint on his SUV and three employees offered to testify to that effect. I was given the largest check I'd seen in six months and as for what happened between Berringer and my client I have no idea and I don't really care. Justice was served and I got the dough. That was good enough for me.

Sometimes being a private eye means putting in a lot of boring, tedious hours to collect a bucketful of mundane and seemingly inconsequential facts. But when all the bits and pieces of data fall into place I feel the same way as when I finish a 2000-piece jigsaw puzzle of the Taj Mahal. It's done, it's pretty, and now it's time to move on to something else.

To celebrate, I went down the street to the "New New York, New York, Pizza Place." The name takes up a lot of space on the window but the pies are hand-tossed, and baked in a brick oven the way God intended. The house specialty is a white cheese and garlic pizza that the people who eat it and everyone they meet within the next 12 hours are able to enjoy to the full. I ordered a medium pie and a cold beer, figuring that garlic is sort of a vegetable, the cheese is dairy, the crust is grain, and the beer is—

well—hops are a sort of grain, too, aren't they? It's my idea of a vegetarian meal.

Wouldn't you know, as soon as I started chewing the last garlicky morsel a very attractive young lady came over to my table, sat down across from me, pulled a piece of paper and a pen from her purse, wrote down her name, address, and phone number, and handed it to me.

"I hope you will give me a call sometime soon. I really need you," she said.

My first thought was that I wished I had stuck a Tic-Tac in my pocket before I left my apartment.

My second thought was, "This has never happened to me before so there must be a catch to it somewhere."

There was a catch. It turned out she hadn't finished talking.

"The guy over at the cash register tells me you're Sherlock Holmes and you solve crimes and things like that. Is that what you are? or was he pulling my leg?"

My third thought was that I would probably enjoy pulling on her leg.

This was quickly followed by a fourth thought, one that noted this was quickly turning into a professional relationship and I had better keep it as impersonal as possible.

My fifth thought was that I was starting to feel like Bob Hope in all those "Road" movies with Bing Crosby. I never seem to get the girl, either.

"Sure, honey," I said in my sleuthiest voice. "I'm Sherlock Holmes and you, I presume, are Dr. Watson?"

When she stared at me blankly I decided I would have to tone down my vocabulary at least one notch if the conversation was going to go anywhere. So I started over.

"Yes, I am a private investigator and I try to find things and solve people's problems. Is that important to you for some reason?"

"No," she said. "I don't need a private—what did you call it—instigator?"

I know what you're thinking but she wasn't. She was a brunette.

The conversation had suddenly veered off the main road and I needed a GPS to figure out where it was going to go next. But she still had more to say.

"I just thought it might be fun to meet an . . . a detective like you. Here's my name and number. Maybe we can meet for coffee. This is so cool. I feel as though I'm hanging out with James Bond. Maybe we can go someplace in your sports car? Are you licensed to kill? Is that a tuxedo under your clothes? Are you working or on vacation?"

At this point, I had my sixth and final thought of the evening: *Of all the gin joints, in all the towns, in all the world, she walks into mine.*

Too bad she wasn't Ingrid Bergman.

At that moment my body tensed with a jerk, my neck muscles straining to keep my head from falling backwards. I realized I must have faded out and fallen asleep somewhere during thought number five.

The girl was still in front of me but she was saying, "Hey, are you okay? Am I boring you?"

Still in a daze, I stammered out, "No, I don't own a sports car. I don't own any kind of car."

After a second or two, my mind cleared enough to tell me I was making an ass of myself.

I needed a quick save but all I could think of was, "Uh, I'm sorry, could you repeat what you said—just that last bit—the acoustics are terrible in here—well? Go on—I'm all ears."

Not much of a save, but at least I had stopped braying.

"Oh," she said. "Sure—the guy who has been making these calls, I reported him to the police, and they told me to just hang up and maybe he would get tired of the game. If he didn't quit and if I felt physically threatened then I should call them back, and they would set up something that would trace his phone number the next time he called. Since then he's called me at least a dozen more times. He hasn't actually threatened me but it's getting to be more than annoying. I deserve to be shown respect, especially in my own home."

I didn't interrupt because the more she kept talking, the more chance I had of catching up with what she was talking about.

When she finally paused, I asked, "What else can you tell me about him?"

"Well, he sounds like a man in his late teens or early twenties. Not stupid-dumb or anything but just immature. The things he says to me make me a little nervous because he seems to know things about me that normal people shouldn't know."

"Like what sorts of things?"

"He seems to know when I wake up, when I go to work, when I get home, and even when I go to bed. It all makes me feel so vulnerable and I don't know what to do. So when I was ordering my pizza and the man told me you were a detective I thought I'd ask you for some advice

48

and see if maybe you were able to help me, you know, with this guy who keeps calling."

I finally felt as though I had got most of her story straight enough to branch out in a new direction.

"Sure, I think I can help you," I said as I slid my business card across the table. "And because you have been so nice about it I'll give you some thoughts for free. First of all, it sounds like he lives close enough to where he can see you come in and out of your building and that he can see enough of your windows to tell when the lights go on in the morning and go off at night. I assume there is a building with windows across the street from your apartment?"

"Yes, but I live on the third floor and when I look out my window most of what I see are the trees that grow along the sidewalk. I suppose he could be looking at me from some of the higher windows. I've thought of that before and it really creeps me out. I've been keeping my blinds and curtains closed almost all the time and I shouldn't have to do that, either."

"Keep doing it. I don't want scare you or anything, but he probably has a pair of binoculars, too. 'All the better to see you with, my dear!'

"I'll tell you what. If you want, I'll go and talk to the manager at the building across the street from your place. I'll tell him we suspect he's got a young man who's being a Peeping Tom. If he knows who lives in the building it shouldn't take very long for him to figure out who it is. If the manager doesn't want to talk to the kid or his family then I'll do it. But that will cost you at least one dinner out. Deal?"

"It sounds like a fair trade to me. But what if the manager does the talking and you don't have to?" she asked.

"Well, then," I said. "I'll be the one who pays for the dinner!"

She smiled and reached her hand out to shake on it, which we did. But I had one final piece of advice to give her.

"I had an elderly friend, a widow who lived alone. She started getting phone calls like the ones you've been getting. The police tried to do all the things they told you they would do, but somehow he kept getting through without being traced. Finally, she got mad enough to step out of her otherwise sugar-sweet personality. The next time he called, she held the phone at arm's length and yelled as loud as she could in the opposite direction. 'Walter, put down that shotgun. I told you the police were taking care of this.' The line went dead, and she never got a call from him again."

She laughed but her smile had already begun to fade.

"Gee, thanks," she said. "If only I had a dead husband it would be perfect! Sure. Give me a call and if something works out then—well—something will work out, okay? No promises, but I'll remember the handshake."

This didn't sound very encouraging but I kept up appearances as best as I could. She stood up, shared the last vestige of her smile, walked up to the cashier, picked up her pizza, paid for it, and left.

A few days later when I had some free time I looked up her address, tracked down the manager of the building across the street, and downloaded the data into his brain. He said there was only one person in the building who fit that description and that he had received complaints about him before from several of the other tenants. He said he would talk to the person and to his parents, and if they owned a pair of binoculars or a telescope he would ask them if they would loan it to him for "safekeeping." I said I would be all right with that but if the complaints continued I might have to take legal action on behalf of my client. He said he understood the concern and assured me he would take care of it and that was that.

In the evening, I phoned the girl to fill her in and to set a date for going out to dinner. When she answered her phone, I filled her in and made a subtle reference to our agreement

"Well," she replied, "I don't know what to say, Mr. Maurison, except 'thank you' for your time and trouble. I need to tell you, though, that I broke my lease and moved out of my apartment this morning. I couldn't take the stress anymore. If I get one more phone call from this guy I'll just change my phone number and start all over. And about that offer for dinner—I know that's what we shook hands on but I'm just getting settled into a new place closer to where I work in East Village. I think I'd better take a rain check, okay? I'm sorry, but that's just the way it has to be this time. Thanks again. Bye."

And that was that.

Me and Bob Hope.

Chapter 4

A Date to Remember

August

Business was booming. Clients were standing in line to get into my office and pay me good money to tail their husbands, find their lost dogs, or track down a missing relative. I admit there is a certain redundancy in putting the words "good" and "money" side by side. After all, the way I look at it, money is good, and anything good usually has something to do with money. If I had a larger vocabulary, I might call it a tautology or the opposite of an oxymoron. But I am not that smart a guy. I am just smart enough to find things for people, which is why the sign on my door says: "Mike Maurison, Private Eye."

Like I said, my finances were rising from the dead faster than Lazarus, but I hadn't had a decent night's sleep in over a week. Dogs and relatives are best located when the sun is shining. Tailing husbands usually means a night out on the town, following a car that looks like every other car on the road. With the exception of Yukons and Tahoes, I've learned to tell the year, make and model of almost any car from the shape and size of its tail lights.

It was 1:30 a.m. and I was so tired I couldn't make it all the way across the apartment to my bed. The sofa was closer so I just curled up in a fetal position and drifted off into a somnambulatory conversation with the cute, brown-eyed girl who sat in front of me in my 10th grade English Class.

I had spent the previous evening shadowing a husband and father of five adolescent children from his home in Greenpoint to Queens. When he pulled into an all-night diner on the Union Parkway I stayed in my car and watched him sit down at the counter, place an order for something, eat it, pay for it, and walk back to his car. He chatted with the waitress but if something was going on between them I must have missed it.

On the drive back he pulled into a service station. I pulled in next to him and we pumped gas together.

Pretending to be friendly I asked, "Why are you out so late tonight?"

I was hoping for a nibble but he took the bait—hook, line, and sinker.

"Just getting away from the wife and kids to keep from going insane," he said. "I can't handle the stress of being pushed around by disrespectful children and a wife who can't cook, and doesn't seem to care whether I'm around the house or not. So, at least one night a week, I do us both a favor and grab some decent food someplace, and make up my mind whether to go back home or not."

I knew our conversation was only going to last a few more seconds so I asked, "Well—what did you decide to do this time?"

He looked me straight in the eyes and said, "I've decided what I always decide to do, and it's the same thing I'll decide to do next week and the week after that. I love my wife and I love my kids. I'm not the best husband or the best father but I'm trying to do the best I can with what I've got. Sure, I need a break now and then but my family is the most important thing in the world to me. It's just not always easy, you know."

He topped off the tank, took his receipt, and drove off in the general direction of Greenpoint. I had seen and heard enough so instead of following him home I headed back to my flat in Upper East Side Manhattan. I wasn't exactly sure what I was going to tell his wife. Whatever it was I was going to do my best to make her husband look as good as possible.

I'm hired to find the truth about things, but most of the time the truth is more complicated than what can be captured on a video cam. If I've learned anything at all in this business it's that truth is better described in poetry than in prose.

I slept better that night than I had in a long time. Maybe it was because I had wrapped up a case. Maybe it had something to do with my dreamland rendezvous with a cute girl. Maybe it was because I was exhausted.

I woke up at 10 o'clock in the morning. It was a bright, clear, sunny Saturday in mid-August, one of those days that moves Manhattan up one notch on the international city scale from "Spectacular" to "It Doesn't Get Any Better Than This." I was tempted to take the day off and do something lazy and selfish but there were precious pets and prodigal sons waiting to be found and returned to their homes and families.

I don't do very well with temptation so, of course, I took the day off.

I removed the clothes I'd been sleeping in, put on some cleaner ones, threw some water on my face, grabbed an over-ripe banana, and hoofed it down to catch the #6 train at Hunter College. I had no idea where I was going until I got to Canal Street, where I decided to transfer onto the N Line to Coney Island.

I sat on the right side so I could catch a clear view of the Brooklyn Bridge as we zipped across the East River. As we passed through Greenwood I wondered how the morning was going for the man I'd tailed the night before. I didn't wonder very long or hard though, because, after all, I was taking the day off.

I don't get down to Coney Island very often. Cotton Candy and roller coasters both make me feel queasy. Not too far from Nathan's Famous Hot Dogs there's a place that sells a decent chili dog—one that always goes down well with a cold beer. I walked the short block from the terminal to the Boardwalk. It was just about noon, so I bought the dog and the beer and sat down next to some guy at one of the few benches that weren't already occupied by what Shakespeare so delicately described as "the infant, Mewling and puking in the nurse's arm."

The guy turned out to be Robert, the security guard at the MoMA. Robert—the man with the stoic face and a lack of verbal skills that would have put old "Silent Cal" to shame. The two of us had what could, literally, be described as a "nodding" acquaintance. The Museum of Modern Art has been my home-away-from-home since I was a kid, so we see each other often enough to be on a first name basis. Or at least we would be, if Robert would quit calling me "Mr. Maurison" instead of "Mike." I guess I consider him to be something like the younger brother I never had.

Except for going out for a beer a couple of times when the museum closed up for the day, I hadn't ever considered the possibility Robert had any sort of life apart from his job. Seeing him sitting next to me on a Coney Island Boardwalk bench on a sunny Saturday seemed as surreal as Dali's *Persistence of Memory,* which at that very moment, was hanging on the wall in the museum's fifth floor gallery.

I tried not to make a big deal out of bumping into him, so I just sat quietly for a moment before saying, "Hi."

Robert didn't make the effort to turn his head away from the beach, but he did say "Hi" in return.

He continued to nibble on a soft pretzel. Like me, he didn't seem to be in any hurry to go anywhere.

When we both finished eating, I stood up, stretched, and asked if he wanted to take a walk on the Boardwalk with me. He gave a non-committal shrug, stood up, and followed me, heading east towards Brighton. To my surprise, Robert looked quite the man, standing tall in an Argyle sweater, blue jeans, and running shoes. Someone else must have thought he was worth a second look, because before we had gone 20 steps, a healthy-looking, less-than-thirty-something girl walking a small black Lab came over, and after a quick glance at me, asked Robert if they had met each other somewhere recently.

Robert offered the usual shrug and added, "I don't know. Maybe."

At that point I became invisible, as Robert's new-found friend chattered on and on about all the places they might have run into each other.

When she finally got around to mentioning the Museum of Modern Art, Robert said, "Yeah. That must have been it. I remember seeing you there on a Sunday morning."

"Oh!" The reply came with a small giggle. "This is such a coincidence. You're the guard at the front door, aren't you?"

Robert gave another shrug, and the girl asked if he had a pen and piece of paper she could write on. He didn't, but I did. I handed her my business card with a pencil. She crossed out all my business information, turned the card over, wrote the name "Chia" along with a phone number, and handed both pencil and card to Robert.

"Give me a call sometime," she said. "Maybe we can get together to talk about art and get to know each other better. Unless, of course," she added as a sort of after-thought, "you're married or engaged?"

The question mark hung, suspended in mid-air, waiting for Robert to do something with it. After a brief moment of suspense, he picked it like Eve picked the apple in the Garden of Eden.

"No," he said. "I'm not," and after a short pause, he added, "What are you doing now? Want a cup of coffee?"

Robert got the girl and he got my pencil. All I got was a small nudge in the side from his elbow as they disappeared into the afternoon crowd, heading west.

As a private eye, I have taught myself how be as invisible as possible. At that moment, standing by myself

58

on the Coney Island Boardwalk on a sunny Saturday afternoon, I figured I had gotten too good at it for my own good. I dropped what was left of my beer in a trash bin and found my way down the steps to the beach.

The sky was turning slate-gray as the afternoon overcast blew in on a cool, North Atlantic breeze. Robert had been smart to wear a sweater. My light windbreaker was no longer doing the job of preventing my teeth from chattering.

I had decided to call it a day when something glimmered in the sand. It came and went so quickly that I couldn't place exactly where it had been. I looked down and around, and finally got on my knees and poked with my fingers. Eventually, I found a small, silver, heart-shaped locket that must have fallen off of someone's necklace. It didn't mean anything to me, but it probably meant something to the person who dropped it.

There was a "Lost and Found" kiosk somewhere, but at that moment, I happened to find myself in the fortuitous situation of being both bored and being a professional seeker and finder of lost things.

What the hell, I said to myself. *Maybe someone's offering a reward if someone finds it.*

Not that I needed a reward . . . Maybe I just needed to do something out of the goodness of my heart for once—just to be nice. They say "good guys finish last." Perhaps that was why Robert got the girl and I got sand in my shoes. But no matter, I decided then and there to do the right and good thing, anyway.

Inside the locket were two faces, cut from photographs and jammed into the little windows that faced each other. One was of a boy who looked to be around 12 or 13 years old. The other was of a young man in his late 20s or early 30s. This was my first clue. The locket probably belonged to a young married woman with a son. There was something etched into the back of the locket. One date was professionally engraved, and read, "2/27/89." Underneath that date, as though it had been scratched with a sharp needle, was another date: "9/11/01."

There was a story here—one that would bring a tear to anyone who has lived in Manhattan—including me. I found myself slipping into poetry when I still needed to keep my focus on the prose. I needed to team up with Joe Friday, and just "stick to the facts." I knew it, but I didn't pay any attention to it. Instead, I looked out across the water at Breezy Point, a small community that, along with the Rockaway Peninsula that connected it to Long Island, had lost more people per capita at the World Trade Center than any other.

In the end, the poetry overwhelmed the prose. The sun gave a last gasp, and disappeared behind the overcast, leaving the beach, the bay, and the peninsula in a darkening shadow. I either shivered or shuddered. I held the locket in my hands as though it was the most precious thing in the whole world, wondering if, for one person at least, it actually was.

I carefully wrapped the locket in my handkerchief and slipped it into my left front jeans pocket. I moved my cell phone over to the right hand pocket with my keys, so nothing would press on the locket. The ride back into Manhattan seemed longer than usual.

Back in my apartment, I took out the locket and opened it. I found a pair of tweezers, set a bright desk lamp on the table, and gently pulled the photos out from their nesting places. On the back of the man's photo were the initials "N. E." On the back of the boy's photo was the name, "Danny."

I searched the Internet for the names of those who died on 9/11. None of them had the initials N. E. The oldest child to lose his life had only been eleven, and none of them had been named Dan or Danny. I was stumped. I listened to my guts, but the only thing I heard was the lingering effects of the chili and beer.

Maybe it was time to pay a visit to my mom, over at the MoMA.

When Picasso painted the famous group of five prostitutes in *Les Demoiselles d'Avignon*, he would never have imagined that one day the middle figure would become the embodiment of my mother. Life, as I had seen more than once that afternoon, was still full of surprises. In any case, it was already 5 p.m,. and since the museum closes at 5:30 on Saturdays, talking to Mom would have to wait until later.

I went to the fridge, found some ham, threw it on a slice of bread along with some wilted lettuce, added some mustard and some ketchup from a bottle that had an expiration date from over a year ago. A second piece of bread turned it into my evening meal. It lasted less than five minutes, leaving me with nothing else to do but plan out my Sunday work schedule and ponder what the locket's photos, names, and dates might mean. There was a clue staring me in the face, but for the life of me, I couldn't see it. So I turned on the T.V.

I can't afford cable or a satellite dish so I have to rely on the airwaves. Fortunately, they still blanket Manhattan like an invisible London fog. A $25 antenna gets me more than twenty-five stations, most of which are broadcast in a language I can understand. I switched on the news.

None of the headline stories interested me, so I left the news anchor droning in the background and picked up the crossword left over from Friday's paper. In some sort of subconscious way, I caught something on the news about the Mayor declaring he wasn't going to sit by and let something go on that he didn't like. There was an on-the-scene report of a fatal car accident that was backing up traffic on Riverside Drive. There was an update on a late season trade between the Yankees and the Astros, and there was a weather report that said tomorrow was going to be warmer, colder, wetter or sunnier than today.

"12-Across" was a five letter word with the clue, "First singer of 'God Bless America.'" I put down the name "Cohen," but it didn't fit with 1-down—a word that was clearly "aspic" from the clue "Dandy in _____." I needed a word that started with an "S," but my mind kept drifting back to the dates on the locket. What else could they mean? A birth? A wedding? An engagement?

I had already forgotten the crossword when my guts kicked in like the *1812 Overture*. What was that news story again? The one about the car accident? Maybe that was the clue.

The folks in and around the World Trade Center would not have been the only people who died in New York that day. There were car accidents, heart attacks, murders and god knows what else. The Internet was useless to test out this theory. The media had been so busy with the unfolding drama of the terrorist attacks that whatever routine obituaries had found their way into

62

print would have been cyber-buried where even Google wouldn't be able to find them.

I spent Sunday knocking on doors in the Village, asking residents and shop owners if they had seen a small, black, Scottish terrier wandering around, and looking lost during the past five days. I had a photo to show them and a stack of flyers that said there was a reward for whoever found the dog and took the time to call my phone number. I asked the store owners if they would post the flyer, and stuck a few of them on some bus stops, even though I knew they would get torn off or covered up within a couple of hours. I have never been very good at finding lost dogs, and even though this didn't seem like it was going to be an exception, I did my best to earn my fee. In any case, I had the $100 retainer up front and already in the bank—the bank I operated out of the silverware drawer in my kitchenette.

Back at my office, I managed to locate the whereabouts of a cocaine-sniffing son-in-law by making a few calls to some friends in the NYPD, and by tapping out a few words on the computer with my index finger. It was easy money I knew would be gladly paid by my desperately-worried client and her daughter.

The next morning, I headed down to the New York Times and leafed through the obituaries starting with September 12. A week or so later, a small item listed the death of Nathaniel Ellerman, 30, a lineman killed while repairing a fallen electrical wire in the Bronx in the early morning hours of September 11. His home was, by a sort of eerie coincidence, listed as being Bayswater, on the Long Island end of the Rockaway Peninsula. He was survived by his wife, Pamela, a son, his parents and a sister. It looked as though my guts had come through for me once again.

It didn't take long to find a telephone listing for a P. Ellerman in Bayswater. I dialed it up and left a short message on the answering machine, along with my number.

I didn't know what sort of message to leave, so I stammered out something like, "Hi, I'm Mike Maurison. I found something at Coney Island today that I think might belong to you. If you could give me a call, you can reach me at . . . ."

Well, you get the idea. I figured the odds were 10 to zero that P. Ellerman would want to give a call-back to a strange voice on her answering machine. But, as I have been so often lately, I was wrong.

At 6:15 that evening, my phone rang.

"Hello," the female voice began. "Is this Mike Maurison who left a message on my answering machine earlier today?"

"Uh, yes it is. Are you Pamela Ellerman?"

"That depends on what you found at Coney Island."

"Before I tell you, I need to know what, if anything, you think you might have lost there. If I tell you first, how do I know you won't claim it's yours whether you lost it or not?"

There was silence for a few seconds, and I thought for sure she was going to hang up. But she didn't.

Instead she replied, "No, I don't think I have ever lost anything at Coney Island. But I think my sister-in-law did two days ago. It was a silver necklace with a heart-shaped locket. Is that what you found?"

Unbelievable. How could this have turned out so well, so quickly?

"Yes," I said with a crack in my voice and a tear forming in my eye. "That is what I found in the beach sand on Saturday afternoon. How can I get it to you or to your sister? I don't want a reward or anything. I just want the owner to get it back. It looks as though it might mean a lot to her."

I could hear what sounded like sobbing on the phone, followed by the sound of someone blowing their nose.

After a few more sniffles, she asked, "Where are you calling from? Where do you live?"

"Upper East Side Manhattan."

"How convenient for you and my sister-in-law," she said. "I can't give you her number but I will give her yours. She'll be glad to hear the news. Thank you so very much. You have no idea how much this means to all of us."

Then there was silence.

Twenty minutes later, my phone rang again.

This time, it was a different female voice that asked, "Is this Mike Maurison?"

"Yes, I am Mike Maurison. Let me guess; you must be Pam Ellerman's sister-in-law."

"I figured," the voice continued, "that you would be expecting me to call about the necklace. Pam told me you found it on the beach at Coney Island. That's where I thought I lost it. I went back on Sunday morning and looked everywhere for it. I went to the Lost and Found, and even asked some of the food and shop owners if anyone had turned it in. I didn't really think I would find it, but I had to try. I've been upset ever since. If you have it I'll be glad to pay you for your trouble."

"No, thanks," I said.

It surprised me how easy it was to turn down the offer of money. It was easy this time, but I didn't want it to become a habit.

"How can I get it to you?" I said. "I'm on the Upper East Side. Is there someplace we could meet?"

"That is so weird."

The voice spoke the words almost as though they were a prayer.

"I live on the Upper East Side, too. Do you know Neil's Coffee Shop at Lexington and 70th?"

"I do. I could be there in 15 minutes. They're open until 9 p.m.. Are you free to meet now?"

"Okay. I'm okay with that. What do you look like and what will you be wearing?"

"Look for the guy with glasses and a red ski hat. I'll wear it just for you."

"You are way too kind. Thank you so much."

In 15 minutes, I was at Neil's wearing my ski hat and looking over the menu. There were more things on it than I could eat if I came in every day for two months. I looked up, and could tell it was her before she even said anything. The fact she was staring at my hat, looking at my face, and looking back at my hat was the only hint I needed.

Her short, dark hair framed a matched set of brown eyes and a smile so beautiful I was half-expecting the world to burst into applause.

"Hi," she said. "Are you Mr. Maurison?"

"Yes, and you can call me Mike. Please call me Mike. And don't be fooled by the ski hat. I've never been skiing in my life and if I did I would probably spend most of the time freezing my backside in the snow."

I groaned silently to myself. How is it that whenever I meet an attractive young woman, my mouth opens up and forgets to shut until I have made a complete fool of myself.

To my relief she smiled more beautifully than before and laughed in a way that made me feel as though I had just been voted "Stand-Up Comedian of the Year."

"Well," she added, "are you going to invite me to sit down or not?"

I hadn't been planning to have dinner with her, or even share a cup of coffee. I figured I would just hand her the locket and shake hands with a "Thank you" or two and a few "fuhgeddaboudits" thrown in until we politely said our goodbyes along with a final "Thank you," and so on.

She led the way to a booth and we sat down across from each other.

She pulled out a menu and said, "I'm hungry. Have you eaten yet? It's still early. Order something. Don't worry, I plan on paying for my own dinner, and you can be sure I won't be paying for yours."

All I could think to say was, "Would you like me to give you the locket? That was all I found, you know. There wasn't a necklace attached to it."

As she waved for the waitress she said, "Of course I want the locket, but whether I get it now or an hour from now won't make any difference. The only thing that matters is you found it. For me, that means taking time out to celebrate."

She ordered a Swiss steak with green peas and pearl onions. I ordered the same burger and fries I always order when I eat at Neil's, which is often because I live just a few blocks away. Neil's is one of the few places where I leave a tip. It's always good to leave a few bridges unburned as you go through life. The tip thing was one reason I jumped at her suggestion to meet there since I was fairly sure I wouldn't end up being tossed out into the gutter.

As we waited for the food she said, "So, tell me about the man who saved my locket from oblivion. And how did you manage to trace it back to me and my sister-in-law?"

It didn't take long to fill her in on the general details: that I was a 30-year old private eye taking a day off, and that my guts figured it all out before I did.

When the food arrived, it triggered something like a green light for her to begin talking in earnest.

She took a bite of meat, and talked and chewed at the same time. I figured she must either be really hungry, or grew up in a home that didn't hold table etiquette in very high regard.

"Yes, Nate was my brother and Danny is his son, who is now 25 years old. He was only ten when the photo was taken. My brother would have been in his early 40s, if he hadn't died. I was born long after he was. He gave me the locket for my second birthday so you can do the math yourself if you really want to. That's the date engraved on the locket. The 9/11 date is what I scratched onto it after he died. That's when I put in the photos of Nate and Danny. So," she paused, either for effect or to catch her breath, "now you can see why that locket is so special to me."

Somehow, while telling me this, she managed to polish off all her steak and most of the pearl onions. I noticed she hadn't touched any of the peas. My burger was gone. I was feeling full, so I offered her some of my fries. She grabbed a few from across the table, and as she nibbled on them, she announced she was ready for me to give her the necklace. I took my handkerchief out my pocket, unfolded it, and handed over the small silver heart that was worth more than gold to her.

She took it gently, almost reverently. She didn't open it. She just turned it over, and over again in her hands, until she gave it a small kiss, folded it back up in my handkerchief, and dropped it into her handbag.

"If you want your handkerchief back, you'll have to give me a call."

She wrote her phone number on a napkin and slid it across the table.

"I already have yours," she added with a smile.

She didn't give me a chance to say anything before she stood up, walked to the cashier, paid for her dinner, and after turning around to give me a final smile and a wave, stepped out onto Lexington Avenue and disappeared into the night.

Someone behind me said, "Closing time. Time to pay up and go home, everybody. Thanks for eating at Neil's."

I did what I was told, thinking maybe Robert and I could go out on a double date sometime.

It had been a long time since I had phoned a girl and asked her out on a date. Even though I tried to pretend otherwise, the last three girls I had taken out to dinner had been clients who wound up picking up the tab for both of us.

On the walk home, I touched the napkin in my pocket and realized I had forgotten to ask what her name was, but that didn't matter. There would be at least one more opportunity to find out. As it turned out, I needn't have worried. Next to her phone number, she had written her name, Mona.

After I walked into my flat and locked the door, I got a funny feeling there was something else I had forgotten to do. As I made my way past the crossword on the dining table, I remembered what it was. I picked up the pen and filled in the word, "Smith."

Chapter 5

A Night on the Town
September

I love Wikipedia. In the old days if you had an argument with a guy in a bar over some piece of trivia such as whether Brigitte Bardot was still alive or not you'd have to call the local library and have the reference librarian look it up for you. The downside to this is that the local library is usually closed when men are arguing about stuff like that in a bar.

That's why I love Wikipedia. If you need an answer in a hurry you can look it up on your computer and cut the librarian some slack. These days if you're in a bar and don't have your desktop computer handy you can use your smart phone or ask the guy next to you to look it up right then and there.

That's what happened to me the other night. I was taking in the scenery and enjoying the ambient décor of Murphy's Saloon & Dive in Tribeca when some guy from

Queens starts in on how Manhattan is where all the wimps go who can't handle a real life with a real job like they do in Queens. That part didn't bother me because, well, after all, he was from Queens and opinions don't bother me. I'm more interested in facts. That's why the next thing he said raised a hackle or two.

"Even the name 'Manhattan' is wimpy," he asserted. "The Indians called it 'Mindanetin' which means 'Land-Between-Two-Rivers' but the Dutch wrote it down as 'Man-hat-in' which, in the local language, means 'cockroach.'"

After a well-timed pause, he added, "And personally, I think the Dutch got it exactly right."

The collective blood pressure in the bar threatened a major aneurism but no one knew whether the guy was telling the truth or not so they just stood there clenching and unclenching their fists looking at one another like umpires do at a Yankees game when none of them saw the play.

That's where Wikipedia came in handy. I've just recently paid for a smart phone, mostly so I can use the GPS to find out where I am and where I'm going, but also to look up stuff I need to know. This was one of those times, so I typed in "Manhattan original Indian name" and up pops a Wikipedia article that proves this lunkhead from Queens is blowing hot air like a heat pump. I lean over to him and, in a whisper, tell him the name "Manhattan" is from the "Munsi language of the Lenni Lenape, meaning 'island of many hills,'" and if he knows what's good for him he should leave as quickly and quietly as possible and get back home to Queens before he's beaten to a pulp by a bunch of wimps.

Fortunately, he takes my advice and the NYPD riot squad is spared having to spend the next three hours in Tribeca.

Why I was sitting in a bar in Tribeca after the libraries had closed is another story.

Ever since we met last month, my new girlfriend, Mona, had wanted to set up a double date with my friend Robert and his new girl, Chia. I suggested we go down to a place called Burger de Bœuf in Tribeca. It's a place I would visit from time to time when business took me to what used to be the New York City Correction Department right around the corner. The food is sort of what McDonald's would be like if Julia Child was the *Chef de Cuisine*.

Everyone thought it was a good idea so we agreed to meet there the following Wednesday to eat at 7:15 p.m. and then try out the "bowl in the dark" gimmick at Bowlmor Lanes near Union Square on the way home.

Mona and I took the subway together and Robert and Chia came separately after they each got off work. We all got there within five minutes of each other, checked out the menu and ordered. Robert looked like a pro sitting there in what looked like a bowling shirt, but instead of having a little stitched picture of falling bowling pins it had something on it that looked like the sort of iron you press your clothes with.

"What's that?" I asked.

Robert answered by saying it was his curling shirt. He added he was in a curling league that had just finished the spring-summer season.

"Curling?" I asked. "That's the Olympic thing where they slide those round granite rocks along the ice like a frozen game of shuffleboard, right?"

Robert said, "Yes."

"What in the world got you doing that? You are full of more surprises than a bowl of *chioppino*."

Robert looked as though he wasn't enjoying being the center of attention, but he tried to be a good sport and answered.

"It's part of my Scottish heritage."

He paused as if he was unsure how much he should share, but after taking a deep breath he opened up like a well-shaken can of beer.

"My Dad taught me how to play before I learned to read. You remember when we ran into each other at Coney Island and I met Chia?"

Chia smiled and rested her head against Robert's shoulder.

"I had just spent the night with my parents in Valley Stream. I grew up there and went to Central High School. My parents are members of the Long Island Curling Club. During the summer, I go curling with my folks on Fridays and then spend the night. It's really easy. I just jump on the E Line that runs right under the Museum on 53rd. It takes me direct to Jamaica where my Dad picks me up. Then we have dinner and go to the Club in Bellmore in time for the 8:00 p.m. match."

Something about curling seemed to turn Robert on like an extrovert on Red Bull. I decided to play with him a little.

"Why is it Scottish men spend so much time doing groin-busting things like heaving boulders, throwing hammers, tossing cabers and sliding heavy stones across the ice? Maybe that's why the birth rate in Scotland has been going down for the last 300 years!"

Robert didn't laugh and Mona glared at me like a laser cutting through titanium. But I hadn't even gotten warmed up yet.

"You know how the Grand Canyon was formed? A Scotsman dropped a penny down a gopher hole! And, wait, you gotta hear this one: Why did the Scotsman cry after tossing a penny to a street musician? Because the string broke! Get it? That's funny!"

Mona gave me a sharp and painful kick under the table but I had too much momentum to slow down.

"Did you hear about the Englishman who drove to Inverness with his Mistress? They wanted to have a highland fling!"

As if it had been choreographed, Robert, Chia and Mona all stood up at the same time and threw their napkins on the table. Robert looked like he was trying hard not to charge me like a credit card but it was Mona who spoke.

"I think the three of us should leave and let Mike enjoy himself for the rest of the evening because no one else is going to."

She nodded at Robert and Chia: "Let's go bowling.""

They didn't even say "good-bye." They just left. The food came and I was stuck with the bill for all four of us. I had ruined a perfectly nice evening, I had mocked the best friend I ever had and felt as low as a contra-bass bassoon.

And that's why I ended up sitting by myself in Murphy's Saloon & Dive.

Even Wikipedia couldn't help me out of this mess. At the saloon, I ordered a Glenfiddich in honor of Robert, but a second whiskey neat wouldn't have solved my problem, either. I had no idea Robert was Scottish. What the hell, after all these years I didn't even know his last name.

The idiot from Queen's had left but I figured I'd stay around, moping and feeling sorry for myself until the place shut down at 4:00 a.m. But I fell asleep at the bar and the barkeep woke me up at midnight and told me to go home before my snoring scared the other patrons away.

One drink hadn't done me any good at all or, for that matter, any bad, either. So I stepped out of Murphy's and started walking the half-mile to the Brooklyn Bridge subway station on the far side of City Hall. Any train from there would get me straight back to the Upper East Side and I thought the chill night air might help me think things over.

A steady stream of sirens blazing past me on Chamber's Street shattered the peaceful, euphoric aura of walking late at night through the dark streets and alleys of South Central Manhattan. I was feeling so bad about what I had said and done that I was almost hoping I'd make atonement for my sins by being mugged. But that wasn't going to happen because in a matter of seconds I was surrounded by cop cars and fire trucks. Alarms started going off in a nearby building and one of the fire trucks shot a beam of light up towards what I figured was somewhere around its 9th or 10th floor.

I expected to see someone standing on a ledge but the light just kept creeping around the front of the building as if looking for something or someone who should be there but wasn't. There was a shout and the light froze in place. A rope, or cable of some kind, had been caught in the beam, fragile-looking and hanging straight down from the top of what must have been at least a 25-story building.

A van with a big blue and white "7" and the words, "WABC Eyewitness News" on the side pulled up and a guy with a camera and a lady in a red dress almost knocked me over as they jumped out. The lady was holding a microphone in one hand and was frantically trying to brush her hair with the other.

Within seconds the cameraman shouted, "Go! You're on!"

A green light gleamed on the camera and a portable spotlight lit the lady up like a human flare. She started talking with the building directly behind her glowing as if everything was being filmed at mid-day rather than at twenty-five minutes past midnight.

"Eyewitness News has just arrived live at Chamber's Street," she said. "Two blocks from City Hall. We have found ourselves in a scene right out of a Gotham City/Batman comic book. Two cleaning women on two different floors of an office building have reported seeing Batman staring into the building from outside. Police and fire trucks are flooding the area with light, searching for whoever was foolish enough to dangle hundreds of feet above hard asphalt and cement. What we'd like to know is what was he doing up there?"

She signed off and headed straight for a fireman wearing a white helmet, the one waving his arms and alternating between shouting though a megaphone and talking on a walkie-talkie.

I have learned that when you can't find something, the second thing you need to do is look for it someplace else. As far as I could see, everybody was looking up in the air and not finding anything except an empty rope. I figured maybe someone should start looking down. I figured that person was going to be me, Mike Maurison — Private Eye.

I fell on my hands and knees and started looking under all the cop cars and fire trucks. There were lots of legs and feet moving about in silhouette with the floodlit building behind them. I turned to look away from the light and noticed something dark and crumpled lying under an ambulance parked off to the side and out of the way.

From under the truck, I pulled a cape and fake leather chest covering with the Batman logo in the middle. I tossed the costume into the arms of a startled EMT and headed away from the building, sprinting south-west on Broadway.

The trees surrounding the City Hall buildings loomed like Mirkwood on my left. I must have headed in the right direction because I picked up something from the gutter that turned out to be a Batman mask and head covering, complete with the little bat ears. I tucked it under my shirt and kept moving toward the closest City Hall subway entrance. There were only a few people walking around at that hour of the night and most of them were scurrying toward the police cars and fire trucks like moths drawn to a light bulb.

I could see one figure moving in the opposite direction. He stood out because it was a chilly, October night and he was only wearing a white t-shirt. He stepped off the sidewalk into the street and started waving franticly for a taxi. One stopped and he got in but the cab just sat there without going anywhere because I was standing in front of it with my right foot planted firmly on the bumper. The driver started blasting his horn and the passenger tried to jump out but I had moved to the side of the cab and when the back door opened and a leg stuck out I pushed the door closed tight against it, pinning the person attached to the leg half in and half out of the car.

The noise of the horn was quickly drowned out by the screaming and swearing of what turned out to be a young woman. She was wearing thick, wool socks and the soft, lightweight shoes preferred by rock climbers. The cabbie got out to see what was going on and I asked him to call a cop. He was glad to do it but figured I was crazy since, as far as he could tell, I was the one who was going to get arrested.

When the NYPD officer arrived, I kept the pressure on the door and showed him my ID as a licensed PI. The cop listened to my story and took a close look at the girl. He took her hand and fixed it to the door handle with a plastic cuff. He then had her stand with her other hand on the roof of the car while he recited the words that made Ernesto Miranda famous.

I had never seen a NYPD officer driving solo in a patrol car at night in Manhattan before. It turned out his partner was just a block away still looking up at the building with everyone else. He joined us in two minutes and took a short statement from me complete with my vital statistics. In return, I handed him Batman's headgear and suggested he put it in a shopping bag or something for safekeeping. He looked annoyed at my condescension but told me to go home and someone would contact me in a few days. I didn't feel optimistic about getting a reward for my heroism. But the thought crossed my mind

I did get some good publicity, though, as the city news media began harassing me for sound bites with my name attached to them. Whatever they said, I agreed with them—which made me out to be more of a hero than I actually was.

Mona, Robert and Chia weren't about to pin any medals on my chest any time soon.

I was too embarrassed to visit Robert at the Museum, and, when I worked up the nerve to give Mona a call the only thing she said was, "Oh, so you're still alive. How nice," and hung up.

I decided to lie low until things settled down, including the acid reflux in my stomach from the angst and stress I was feeling. I needed a distraction and I found it when I opened my mail on Monday afternoon.

The letter was addressed to "Mr. Mike Maurison" and looked like a formal invitation to a wedding, an art gallery opening, or a soirée. It was an invitation to a "Celebration of the Prodigal's Return" issued by a client of mine in Greenwich Village who had misplaced her Scottish terrier back in August. I'd put out posters and later gotten a phone call from someone who thought they had found it. I called my client, someone got a reward, I got paid (handsomely) and now I got this invitation to a party in the dog's honor.

This dame was not living on a tight budget like I do, and over the years, I have buttered my bread more than once by smooching, groveling, and otherwise selling myself out to the upper crust, so I RSVP'd I'd be there at 7:30 p.m. sharp on Friday.

I figured I might as well celebrate too. After all, I had never actually helped anyone find a dog before.

Between then and the party I worked on a few cases that had fallen through the cracks. One thing I often do is investigate small crimes the police don't have the time or inclination to worry much about. This does not usually elicit a positive, upbeat, cop-friendly response from the victim, so when clients come in to see me I sometimes have to spend the first fifteen minutes or so listening to them vent their anger at the NYPD. They tell me how unfair it is since they pay taxes for years and when the time comes when they actually need help from the police all they get is a "Sorry, ma'am. All we can do is write down a list of what was taken and, if any of it turns up, we'll let you know."

I have never yet heard of anyone who was notified that something on his or her list had turned up. The black hole for stolen goods in the Big Apple must be getting as full as the landfill outside of Trenton.

So this lady comes into my office. She is smartly dressed in a dark gray wool maxi-skirt and a heavy blue satin blouse covered by a thigh-length black-knit, button-up sweater. The black Cossack boots and black faux alligator handbag completed the ensemble. Long black hair, soft red lipstick and a hint of dark blue mascara framed the face of a young lady in her mid-twenties. She was the type who smiled and winked and giggled as though she was flirting for no reason other than having an uncontrollable compulsive disorder. She was playful, but in a very distracting and annoying sort of way.

81

"Hi, there," she breathed steamily, "you big, strong, handsome man. Just the sort of private eye I need . . . desperately."

Since I am average height, above-average weight, wear glasses, and stopped paying my membership dues at 24-Hour Fitness years ago, the thought crossed my mind the lady could have used a pair of glasses herself.

She wasn't done.

"My life and New York's finest have been big disappointments to me lately as I am sure you'll understand, given the exotic, dangerous and mysterious line of work you are in. I know I am not the first tearful woman who has come into your office with a sad story to tell, but tell you I must. It is a story the police were unwilling to pause for even a few, paltry minutes to hear. So now I am reduced to paying someone to listen to me, console me, and, I hope, solve and resolve the injustice I have been forced, against my will, to endure."

I looked around the room to see if there were cameras, a director or maybe a scriptwriter hovering somewhere in the shadowy corners of my office. The scene was straight out of what would have been the worst *film noir* ever made. I'm no Humphrey Bogart and this dame was no Mary Astor, but I figured if there was a plot that involved me getting paid to do something then I was willing to be type-cast as Sam Spade.

I did my best to fill the role by saying, "Okay kid, if you've got something to say, then I've got ears to hear it. Give it to me with both barrels."

And that is exactly what she did.

The story she told was so outrageous it verged on entertainment. It was parody, farce and melodrama all rolled into one big Tinsel Town B-movie theatrical production. The word "emote" did not do justice to what I was hearing. "Gushing" would be more accurate.

Finally, after I had spent 10 minutes trying to keep from exploding into hysterical laughter she reached a dramatic pause and then brought down the house with the *denouement*: "I am heartbroken and near to death from the pain and loss I have suffered in this catastrophic case of criminal audacity. They took it, I want it back, and I will pay you a king's ransom if you can find and return my precious . . . stuffed bird of prey."

"It wouldn't by any chance happen to be a falcon, would it?"

I allowed myself to break into a smile.

"Well," she paused again for effect, "as a matter of fact . . . ."

The dame was interrupted in mid-sentence when my office door flew open and Mona, Robert, and Chia walked in. Mona was carrying a ratty stuffed parrot, which she solemnly set down on my desk. We all cracked up and never before was I so glad to have been set up as a fool.

Chia pulled a bottle of chilled champagne from a bag along with five plastic cups while Robert poured and offered a toast: "To the biggest jerk and best friend in the world. Cheers."

The "dame" turned out to be named Cherise, a friend of Chia's who had moved to New York in the hope of breaking into the theater business. She had played her role perfectly, and if she ever needed a reference letter, I would write one, have it notarized, and have it delivered anywhere in the world overnight if it would help her get a job.

Robert was wearing his curling shirt and a kilt, Mona tossed a British penny onto my desk, and Chia did a very bad imitation of a highland fling. It was perfect and the tears in my eyes were not necessarily from laughing so hard. The crumpled handkerchief I keep in my left front pocket emerged into daylight and was returned a few moments later as damp as a sub-basement in New Orleans. It seems they had gotten the parrot at Thor's Pawn Shop down the street and, in the spirit of Dashiell Hammett, it was filled with half a pound of fake diamonds. Did I say it was perfect? I hope so, because it was.

Mona graciously agreed to be my date at the dog party on Friday, and on Saturday, the three of them treated me to dinner at Burger de Bœuf. We didn't go bowling, but Robert made me promise I would go curling with him one night at the Ardsley Curling Club in Irvington which was open year 'round while the Long Island Club was closed for the autumn-winter season.

A few weeks later, I did go curling. I strained my back lifting the curling stone the wrong way and spent the next three days popping pain pills and lying on my sofa watching old Humphrey Bogart movies.

I have since taken an oath I will never make a joke about Scotland again, and my respect for the sport of curling is now the stuff of legend.

Chapter 6

Masks
October

October always makes me think of Halloween which makes me think of pumpkins which make me think of Cinderella. I can't help it. My brain has been set on free-association auto-pilot since I was in elementary school. If someone mentions they have recently been to the Statue of Liberty, the image of a Japanese *tatami* mat will pop into my head because it would be a "low bed" which is a mirror image of the word Bedloe; the name of the island the Statue of Liberty was built on. And if someone mentions that it has been a great season for catching tuna then I will immediately recall the joke about the musical fish who fixed pianos. He was, of course, a piano tuna.

Most people think that someone whose thoughts randomly ricochet like laser beams in a video game must be on drugs or under some kind of a curse. Although I sometimes misdirect an otherwise perfectly good conversation and sometimes cause people to groan and throw things at me, I can't say I have any regrets. In one sense, I provide myself with a built-in entertainment system, like playing solitaire with words. In another sense, I confuse the heck out of psychologists when they make the mistake of giving me a Rorschach inkblot test.

The key word in all of this is, of course, "Cinderella." I suppose her real given name must have been Ella and she got the rest of it because she was forced to sweep the floors and clean out the chimney. Then again, I wonder if she had been a milkmaid would she have been called Udderella? Or if she had been an Italian pizza chef would she have been named Paella? But, as usual, I digress.

I guess I just enjoy rags to riches stories, especially when there are evil people around who are archetypically terrifying but who repent, suffer some retributive fate, or are obliterated entirely by the end of the story. After all, that is part of my job as a private eye—to find the truth in a mass of red herrings so justice can be served, the wicked can be punished, and the oppressed victim can turn into a princess and live happily ever after.

Unfortunately, in the real world in which I live and move and have my being I have reluctantly come to the conclusion that frogs are only what they appear to be— frogs. I have kissed a few in my time and I have yet to see even one of them turn into a princess. I suppose that is why Halloween has a certain appeal to me.

Other holidays are bright and cheery, like Christmas, Easter and Thanksgiving. They are nice in their own way, but do not reflect life the way I know it.

Halloween, on the other hand, is like real life: dark and dangerous, sinister and creepy-spooky, full of frightening things that go bump in the night. A lot of the cases I investigate do not have happy endings. Evil triumphs and prospers, innocent people suffer and die, and, as for folks like me who try to do the right thing, we get the rags and the bad guys always seem to get the riches. There are treats, of course. But the tricks are there, too. Real life . . . Halloween.

Sometimes I just want to give it all up and spend the rest of my life going curling with Robert or sitting in the Met Museum contemplating *Aristotle Contemplating a Bust of Homer*. The only thing that keeps me in the investigation business is the fact that deep down inside I am a bull-headed optimist. Somehow, in spite of all the evidence to the contrary, I believe Job and other people who suffer unjustly will one day get their day in court and be vindicated.

Mona feels the same way, but because she goes to church her optimism is all wrapped up in God putting an end to sin and evil at some point down the line. She says that because of Easter you can't be a Christian without being an optimist. If she is right, then I have known a lot of folks who called themselves Christians but had apparently missed the punch line.

The words "punch line" made me think of a bunch of people at a party holding out empty cups at the beverage table, and thinking about that made me feel thirsty. So I rang up Mona to join me for a cup of coffee at Neil's during her morning break. She said she had already arranged to meet Chia there so would I mind if there were three of us? I don't know how she does it, but no matter how thin Mona spreads herself she always seems to have more than enough left over for me.

So, of course, I said, "Sure."

They were already sitting in a booth when I arrived. I ordered my coffee as thick and black as they could make it and the girls each ordered an Italian Soda. After the mandatory ritual of "Hi, how-are-you?" Chia started talking about this old lady she sees every day walking up and down the sidewalk in front of the beauty salon where she works.

"She looks so sad and worn out and she carries these large plastic bags around with her. I guess they hold her clothes or maybe stuff she thinks she can recycle. I don't know but it just kills me to see her walk by the window while I am giving the full spa treatment to a lady who, if they switched clothes like the *Prince and the Pauper*, I wouldn't be able to tell one from the other."

Being the wise, thoughtful, insightful and considerate man I am, I broke in and said, "Yep, that's the way it is, isn't it? All these people living on the street. Maybe it would be a good idea to build a big place for them up in Albany and bus them all out of Manhattan. I think everybody would be happy with that."

Mona and Chia stared at me as if to let me know I had missed the target by a couple of light years. Then Mona picked up where Chia had left off.

"I know what you mean," she said. "Every woman likes to be pampered once in a while and to feel special and beautiful. That's why you do such a good business even when the economy is falling as flat as pancake makeup."

I couldn't help but smile to see some of my wordplay creeping into Mona's conversation. Hanging out with me has changed Mona a little but hanging out with Mona has changed me a lot. Maybe that's why this crazy idea popped into my head like the nose of a camel poking into the proverbial tent.

"Why don't we all chip in and buy her one of those spa treatments? You know, with the hair makeover, the mudpack with the cucumber things, the hair removal, the manicure, the pedigree, you know, the whole hog-on-a-spit."

To my surprise, the girls didn't stare back at me with their mouths hanging open in disbelief. Instead, Chia actually looked as though she was listening to my contribution to the conversation with the same respect as she did Mona's. Mona pointed out I probably meant to say "pedicure" instead of "pedigree" but she also said she thought my idea sounded like a good one.

"Maybe we can't change her life forever," she said, "but maybe we can at least change it for one day."

I have noticed men need to spell everything out in detail when they're making plans but women seem to understand each other even when the words don't make any sense to me at all. This was one of those times. No one said, "Should we do this?" or "What do you think?" or "What do you think she would think?" or "How much would it cost?" or things like that. Whatever questions might have seemed important to me appeared to have been settled between the two ladies at the table without another word being spoken.

Without wasting another moment, Chia simply said to Mona, "If I see her this afternoon I'll set it up and let you know."

She then turned to me and said, "Wow, what a nice surprise. You actually came up with a good one!"

Several hours later I was still trying to figure out whether that was a compliment or not. I'm sure Mona knew exactly what Chia meant. Women are the one mystery even Mike Maurison, Private Eye, will never be able to figure out.

Mona and Chia left for work before I had a chance to finish my second cup of coffee.

From out of nowhere the image of a large semi-truck emblazoned with the words, "Extreme Makeover" came into my head. Hundreds of people are standing around anxiously waiting to see what is behind it. Millions of people are sitting on the edge of their seats with their eyes glued to their TVs watching the same drama unfold. The moment is, of course, shattered by a long commercial break but when the ads are over, the cameras cut back to the truck that slowly, ever-so-slowly, rolls out of the way to reveal an ordinary looking middle-aged woman standing on a small platform, shading her eyes from spotlights that are making her carefully-coiffed hair and airbrushed skin gleam like teeth in a toothpaste commercial.

If I had been asleep, I might have classified this as a nightmare, but since I was wide-awake and knew it wasn't really happening, I was able to write it off as a side effect from being over-caffeinated.

A glance at my watch warned me I was about to be late for an 11:30 a.m. appointment back in my office. I dropped some cash on the table to cover the drinks and the tip and hurried back to do what I do for a living.

I found a young man in his early twenties waiting for me. I opened the door, invited him in, and after we both settled into our chairs, I asked him what was on his mind.

He managed a smile but it looked as though it took some serious effort to pull it off.

"I'm here because of my wife—No, I don't mean that. I mean I'm here because something happened to my wife and I'm hoping you can help."

It was a good snack but it needed more ingredients before it could become an entrée.

"I see," is what I said in response. "Go ahead and fill me in on the details."

His story explained why he had such a hard time raising a smile.

"Tina and I have been married for three years. We fell in love in high school and I have never looked at another girl since—at least not in the way I look at Tina. We're both employed and we have our own apartment about 20 blocks north of here. Everything was perfect until four months ago when some crazy guy decided to throw acid into her face while she was waiting for a bus.

"The guy got away, but Tina spent the next six weeks in the hospital being treated for severe burns on her face and neck. Half of her face still looks like its been rubbed raw with sandpaper and she lost some of the vision in her left eye. We've had counseling about it but we hardly speak to each other anymore. She says she hates herself and doesn't believe it when I tell her I still love her.

"'How can you love me?'" she says. "'Just look at me!'"

"She hasn't left the apartment since she came back from the hospital except for visits to see the doctor and for our counseling appointments. She says she doesn't want to see the counselor again and is about ready to quit on the doctors, too. She says she just wants to disappear and die—as if that would make me happier or something."

I tried to imagine what he and Tina had been going through and the thought made me feel sick. A year ago it wouldn't have bothered me, but now, with Mona in my life, his story homed in on me like a cruise missile, up close and personal.

I swallowed hard and said, "What do you need me for? I'm a private eye, not a doctor or a psychiatrist. You need to have Tina checked for depression right away. What you've said really worries me."

"It worries me, too," he replied. "In fact, it terrifies me. It's like waking up from a nightmare and having the nightmare follow me around even when I'm awake, haunting and taunting and mocking everything that has ever meant anything to me. But no, I didn't come here thinking you could fix this for us. We've got all the professional help we need and somehow we'll manage to survive—somehow—I don't know how but we will."

I keep a box of tissues on my desk for moments like these. After this appointment, I figured I would have to buy another box.

"So," I tried again. "How can I be of help?"

After taking a deep breath, he answered by saying, "Oh, I don't think I even told you my name. I'm sorry. I haven't been thinking straight for a long time. I'm Sean. Sean Strachan."

After an awkward pause when both of us felt we should shake hands but neither of us initiated it, Sean continued.

"This is the thing. The guy who stole my wife's face also stole her purse. In it were my wife's wedding and engagement rings. She's a nurse's aide and the rings catch on the gloves she has to put on and take off all day. That's why they were in the purse instead of, well, you know, on her hand. Anyway, there was also some money but that doesn't really matter. The police took a report and got a description of the guy and they even had a fuzzy photo of him taken from the bus stop security camera. I guess they did what they could but nothing ever came of it.

"I think losing the rings has hurt Tina almost as much as the acid did. Somehow the rings connect her to the way things were . . . before . . . well . . . before she was attacked. I think she feels as though her past was stolen from her along with her future. I'm hoping maybe you can pick up where the police investigation left off. Can you do this? Do you think you can track down this guy and . . . ."

He had been looking me in the eye but now he dropped his gaze down to the floor.

"I know, I know," he said. "It's useless. The rings are long gone and who knows where this guy is or how you would ever find him. I'm sorry to have wasted your time. Tina made me promise to try something and so—well—I guess I did it for her. I'm sorry. I guess that's it. I'll go now. Thank you for listening."

He stood up to leave but I couldn't just let it go like that. After all, I had just been thinking about what a die-hard optimistic crusader for justice I was. Anywhere else in the world, this case would have been considered as being impossible. Here in Manhattan, a happy outcome would be considered as being even less likely than that.

One of Mona's favorite things from the Bible is where it says something like, "I can do anything because with God nothing is impossible." I think I have the quote garbled up, but that's the way it has stuck in my brain. Hanging around Mona isn't turning me into a biblical scholar but a lot of what I've heard makes sense even though it doesn't make sense—if that makes any sense—I don't know. But anyway, I figured if God could do it then maybe I could, too.

The logic didn't really add up but I told Sean I would take the case and only charge a fee if I came up with something. Sean stared at me as if I had just lost my mind but managed to give me his personal information and the case and file number from the police investigation to which, as his contracted agent, I would have legal access. Before he left we shook hands, and without being forced, the hint of a smile flickered on his face.

After getting some paperwork signed by Sean, Tina, and some other people who needed to be involved, I was able to take a look at what was in the police file. There was a police sketch of some thuggish-looking, generic young man wearing the traditional and stylish knit cap and dark glasses. There was a small moustache and a fringe of unkempt hair, neither of which meant anything since the guy could have cut, grown, reshaped or re-colored it a dozen times since the attack. There was a mark on the neck that Tina had described on the report as looking like the end of a bat's wing, or maybe a dragon's wing curling out from under the neckline of his jacket. The fuzzy security photo didn't add anything of use except for confirming that the guy was wearing the cap, a hoodie, and that he was physically able to run without falling down.

The attack took place across the street from Mt. Sinai Hospital where Tina had just finished her shift. But the

94

guy could have been from anywhere, so that wasn't much of a clue either. The police had sent out the usual description of the rings to Manhattan jewelers and pawn shops but that was useless, too, since all the thug needed to do was put the rings in an envelope and send them to somewhere like Fallon, Nevada, in return for a few bucks cash.

I made my customary stop to see Thor at his pawn shop on the corner down from my office. He showed me every set of rings he had, as if to make it clear nothing in his store was hot, so far as he knew. He did say there was a guy who specialized in collecting pawned or otherwise misplaced rings up in Washington Heights. The man was legit and let the police look through them if they needed to. He usually held onto the rings for a while just in case someone came looking. Then he would sort out the ones that had little value for resale, separate the gemstones from the precious metal, and send them down to a jeweler on West 47th Street to be recycled.

Thor gave me the man's address and phone number. I gave him a call, got on the subway and met him at his place in less than an hour.

He had a walk-in safe in the back of his shop, and when he opened a drawer the size of a large safe-deposit box, the room sparkled like Smaug's Lair in *The Hobbit*.

I gave him the description of the stolen rings and he said that without a picture it would be a waste of time to look.

"There are probably a hundred sets of rings in this drawer that match your description," he said. "Unless someone knew exactly what they were looking for, they wouldn't be able to tell one from the other."

95

It occurred to me that it was just like the *Prince and the Pauper* thing again. No doubt in the book the two mothers could have said which kid was which and that thought, of course, led me to take the next step.

"Don't do anything until I get back up here with the person who lost the ring."

The man shrugged and said he could stand there and do nothing for a day or two but after that he would have to go back to making a living.

I expected to wince when I first saw Tina the next morning, but if it wasn't for Sean's emotional description of her face, I would have just figured she had gotten a bad sunburn. Even so, I knew it wasn't a sunburn and I knew it probably was not going to go away anytime soon. If she had smiled, she would have looked even more beautiful than she already did.

At 10:00 a.m., the three of us walked into the ring shop. Within two minutes, the first handful of rings had been strewn across a large, well-lit piece of dark-blue velvet like the ones in a jewelry shop. Tina kept picking up rings and setting them aside. Her hands were so sweaty she sometimes had to shake them before the rings would drop off.

The only thing she said was, "Oh, I hope these aren't all stolen like mine were. I never dreamed there could be so many people . . . hurting . . . like me . . . ."

While rummaging through the fifth handful of rings God stepped in and did the impossible. At least that is the only explanation I could think of at the time. Tina picked up a ring with a small solitaire diamond surrounded by a half-dozen diamond chips and started sobbing. Sean took the ring from her and looked inside where the letters "S &

96

T" had been microscopically engraved. There was no doubt this was her ring. If Tina had been foolish enough to have prayed for me to intercede with God on her behalf then I would now be qualified for beatification by the Vatican. Even the shop owner said it was a miracle. In all his years as a dealer, he had never ever had anyone find a missing or stolen ring in his inventory.

After the sobbing had stopped, Tina picked up where she had left off, looking for the wedding band that was still missing. In the end she had to accept the fact that even if she looked through them a thousand times she wasn't going to find it there.

Another Bible verse came to mind that I had known even before I met Mona. "Seek and ye shall find." As far as I was concerned, this proved it. After all, if we hadn't searched we wouldn't have found anything! I guess if you never attempt to do the impossible you will never really know whether it is impossible or not.

In spite of declaring the whole thing to be a miracle, the owner was a businessman at heart. He said that since there was no way for them to prove the ring was really theirs they would have to pay him for it. They gladly paid him what he asked, but it was clear to every one of us he had let them have it for far less than it was actually worth.

Sean and Tina's subway stop came before mine, but they insisted I walk with them over to their apartment. Inside, the curtains had been pulled shut, making the place look as closed and claustrophobic as a jail cell. Sean made no effort to pull them open, as if darkness and shadows had become a routine part of their lives.

But Tina, who had said very little all day, walked across the living room to the window, pulled the curtains wide open and said, "I hadn't noticed how gloomy it has been in here. It's time we let some light back into our lives."

She smiled at Sean and she smiled at me. I could no longer see the scars on her face. I could only see the radiant beauty of youth, overflowing with a joy, a peace and a love that had been hidden for a time but never stolen. Tina asked if I would like to have lunch with them. I said I would like that very much. The tuna sandwich she fixed for me was the sweetest meal I had eaten in a long time.

When it came time for me to leave, Sean handed me an envelope with my name on it. I peeked inside and saw a small wad of cash. After a moment's thought, I separated out half and handed it back to him.

"Here you go," I said. "Consider this to be a part of my investment in your new future. If you want, put it towards the cost of a new wedding ring for Tina."

Normally I would have considered myself to be as lucky as hell to have found a ring like this. But I had a feeling in my guts that maybe, just maybe, there was something else going on that I couldn't quite put my finger on.

When I got back to my office I realized I hadn't checked my voice mail all day. I did and found one from Mona telling me Chia had set up an appointment with the street lady for tomorrow morning at 10:30 and it would be really nice if I could be there to see how it all turned out. So I phoned her back and said, yes, I would like that, and thanks for letting me know.

The salon where Chia works is down in the Village. I got there at 10:00 a.m., just in time to catch up on some things with Mona. She was really happy to hear the story about the ring. I couldn't tell for sure but I thought I caught her take a quick glance at the ring finger on her left hand. But, like I said, I might have been mistaken.

Chia said the lady's name was Maria Marquez and she was from the Dominican Republic. Her husband left her years ago but she had three grown children who try to keep in touch and who have offered to take her into their homes, but she just wants to be on her own. So she stays in shelters or friends' apartments during the cold months and camps out with some men friends during the warmer months. She feels safe and protected but sometimes she feels lonely. Her English is not very good but it turns out Chia speaks Spanish like a pro which really came in handy during her conversation with Maria.

When Chia asked her if she would like to get the royal treatment at the beauty salon she shook her head and said, "No. I could never afford that, and even if I could, I would rather spend the money on my friends. They need it more than I do."

In response, Chia told her it wouldn't cost Maria anything, but no one was going to give her any money.

Chia said Maria chewed on that for a long time before saying, *"Si,"* and *"Gracias."*

After they had set up the appointment, Maria went off down the street carrying the familiar plastic bags filled with treasures known only to her.

10:30 a.m. came and went, and after 15 more minutes, we were ready to accept the fact Maria wasn't going to show up. But to our pleasant surprise, she did. She had obviously prepared for her visit. Her hair looked as though it had been washed, brushed and tied back with a blue ribbon. She smelled like Dial Soap and her clothes, while still somewhat shabby and worn, looked as though they had also been recently washed. She did not wear any makeup, but after looking at her more closely, I could tell she had once been a very attractive woman. I could also see that the beauty was still there, waiting to be released from all the years of wear and tear on the street.

Chia said some words in Spanish that I didn't understand and Maria followed her across the room to a chair and sat down. A woman came over and began working on her hands and nails. When that was done she started all over again with her feet. After that, they did some things I had to ask Mona about. Not being a metrosexual I had never been inside a woman's beauty salon before and was totally mystified by the whole scene. They put up a curtain while they did some things to her legs, arms and body. Mona said they were going to do the full facial treatment as well so I wound up being there a lot longer than I had planned.

I had never realized how much time, money, and effort women put into looking as nice as possible. I had always thought Mona looked good because . . . well . . . just because she looked good. When I asked her how much time she spent in beauty salons she laughed and said the only thing she did was get her hair cut and styled every other month. The rest of her, with the exception of some lipstick, eye shadow, a little rouge and earrings, was just the way God made her—helped along by maintaining a healthy diet, taking long walks and visiting the gym for two hours every week on the days she had off when I was working.

After a while, Maria emerged from behind the curtain. She looked different—not just her face and hands but everything about her had been transformed. She looked relaxed and almost regal in the way she held her head. She wasn't smiling, exactly, but it was clear from her eyes she was enjoying the experience immensely and taking great pleasure in being pampered. Chia had spoken with her to make sure her hair would be done the way she wanted. It was washed, cut and styled in what seemed to me to be an old-fashioned Latin style, pulled tight, similar to the way she had worn it when she had walked in.

When it was all over, she stood up and turned to Chia with a big smile. Chia and Mona began the applause and soon everyone in the salon, including me and the other patrons, joined in. Maria had become *"Queen for a Day,"* and although tears didn't exactly pour down her face, her eyes did glisten and sparkle as though she were a small girl seeing her presents under the tree on Christmas morning. She said *gracias* over and over so many times it became embarrassing for Chia, who looked as if she hadn't thought about how to wind the whole thing down when it was all over.

Eventually Maria looked in the mirror one last time, gently touched her hair and then, with a final *"Gracias,"* walked out of the door and back onto the streets. On that day, at least, there had not been a plastic bag in sight.

After Maria left, Chia looked at Mona, Mona looked and me, and I looked at Chia. Then, in the way women do and men don't know how, Mona and Mia burst into laughter at the same time.

When they had calmed down Chia said, "That turned out well, didn't it?"

Mona added, "Yes, and she looked so beautiful."

Then they both turned to me and said, "Great idea, Mike. Thanks."

Then Chia had to go back to work.

After a hug, Mona said good-bye to Chia and joined me in getting back to the Upper East Side in time to do some work before the sun set. I couldn't help but wonder what Maria was going to do tonight. Mona said not to worry about it, that Maria was a big girl and could take care of herself.

Two days later, Chia said she had seen Maria walking past on the far side of the street. Chia had waved and said, "Hi, Maria," but she just kept on walking as though she hadn't heard a thing. Chia said even though she still looked better than before she had come in, she would probably revert to her old appearance within a few days. Even so, for one glorious morning, she had been young again and beautiful. Like the credit card commercial says, the whole experience was "priceless." And not just for Maria, but for us, too.

I suppose there are thousands of Cinderella stories being played out in Manhattan every day. After thinking about it, it crossed my mind that maybe, just maybe, I have been wrong about Halloween. I had believed that our every effort to be good, and honest and true was, in the end, little more than a gossamer mask projecting a false reality fueled by futile dreams and wishful thinking; a feel-good illusion designed to hide, obscure and distract us from the real world of darkness and terrifying evil represented by Halloween.

But now I'm beginning to think that maybe it is the other way around. That maybe Halloween and everything it stands for is the real mask, an illusion somehow summoned up to hide, obscure, and distract us from an even greater reality of goodness, beauty and love; a reality that, when all is said and done, will triumph in the end.

Mona has a Bible verse hanging on the wall of her bedroom that says, "The light shines in the darkness and the darkness will never put it out." I suppose light and darkness could go back and forth forever like the perfect balance of the Yin and Yang. But my guts tell me otherwise.

My experience with Tina and Maria taught me something else about life in general and about Halloween in particular. Pumpkins can indeed turn into magic carriages, frogs can turn into Kings and Queens, and what we see on the outside is not necessarily what is hidden underneath. Behind every Darth Vader costume is a potential Prince Charming. And beneath every Fairy Princess costume is, of course, a Fairy Princess.

Chapter 7

Thanksgiving
November

I don't know why Mona keeps hanging around with me. I doubt it has to do with any animal magnetism on my part. The only animal magnetism I have ever had is for dogs. Over the years I have had seven or eight of them like me so much they wanted to take a piece of me home with them. Now, whenever I see a "Beware of Dog" sign I call my medical insurance carrier and ask for preauthorization before I go in.

It was just after Halloween. The bookstore where Mona works had thrown a party for the staff, along with their family and friends. Mona had said I could either pretend to be part of her family or I could pretend to be her friend. Either way she wanted me to come. I poked her back by saying I didn't need to pretend I was her friend, but pretending to be part of her family might be too much for me to manage at this point in our relationship.

"So, then," she said, "It's agreed. You'll come as my friend."

Mona has this bad habit of making up my mind before I do and sometimes I agree with her but sometimes I don't. This was one of those "don't agree" moments.

"I thought this whole thing was about pretending," I replied. "Why don't we just pretend I pretended to say 'Yes' and then I pretended to dress up as King Kong and pretended to go to your party and pretended to climb up on top of your manager's desk and pretended to wave a model airplane around in my hand. Afterwards, when we pretended we got home, we could pretend we had a good time."

She bit me back like one of my doggie pals by saying, "Maybe we should go back to where we were pretending you were my friend. Right now I could buy into that scenario without any problem at all. That way you only have to pretend to be my friend while we're at the party. Afterwards things can go back to the way they are now."

"Mona," I said. "I'm sorry but you know I don't like going to parties. And it shouldn't surprise you to learn I don't like to wear costumes either. To me it's just silly."

So Mona went to the party by herself and I'm still trying to pretend she wasn't seriously disappointed in me.

As I think about it, I just said something that wasn't quite correct. Instead of saying there have been "seven or eight" dogs that have fallen in love with my pound of flesh I should have said, "eight or nine". The statistics changed early one Monday evening at Neil's Coffee Shop while Mona was chewing on her Swiss steak and talking at the same time. She was telling me just how much fun the

106

Halloween Party had been without me and maybe it would be fun for her to do more things without me in the future. I wasn't sure where this conversation was going but I was hoping Mona would at least let me go along for the ride. I'd spent most of my life spending time with myself. It wasn't much but back then it was all I had. With Mona, I had started to look forward to things; especially things that involved being with her. *Dammit,* I said to myself. *I don't want Mona to have fun without me. I want me to be her fun.*

As often happens when I try to say something about girls, even my unspoken words come out sounding stupid. Maybe that is one reason I have learned to talk silently to myself as often as possible.

Anyway, while Mona was sorting out her pearl onions from the peas my phone rang. The call was from a former client I had once helped to repair a broken toilet. That had been in the days before my professional reputation had climbed from zero to negligible. Back then, I had to take whatever work I could get. Now that I think of it, that part of my professional life hasn't changed very much.

The guy's name was Mo and he had rediscovered my business card while looking for a paper clip in his desk drawer. He was calling on behalf of his next door neighbor, a man who had told Mo he had been burgled on Halloween. The neighbor didn't know whether to report it to the police or not and wasn't sure what he could do to get some money back from his insurance. Apparently there was some sort of complication and Mo thought a private investigator might be able to help sort it out.

"Sure," I said. "I'll take the case. When do you want me to come over?"

107

"How about now?" he suggested.

"Now?" I groaned. "Like this evening?"

"Yeah, that's what I said. I'm glad to know that your ears are still working. You know where I live. I'll see you in about thirty."

Mo is as straight arrow as they come; salt of the earth, tell-it-like-it-is and no beating around the bush. In short, he is as annoying as hell, but since I didn't have anything on my calendar until the next afternoon, I looked across the table at Mona and said, "Duty calls."

She waited until she popped the last pearl onion into her mouth before saying, "When I was a kid I had a dog who did his duty on the living room carpet. Where are you going to do yours?"

As usual, I did my best to ignore the sarcasm and simply gave her the back story and filled in the half of the conversation she hadn't heard.

"Sounds like fun," she said. "Can I go with you?"

She gave a sly, suggestive smile and started batting her eyes.

"If you let me come I'll take back all that stuff I said about having fun doing things without you. Deal? or no deal?"

Usually I would have laughed her off as tactfully as possible, but the night was still young, the case seemed fairly innocuous and anyway, I had been trying to think of something we could do that wouldn't cost us an arm and a leg. In Manhattan you can't even buy a slice of pizza without it costing at least a leg.

So I said, "Sure, why not. Let's do it."

We got up, walked to the cashier, paid for the food and limped over to the bus that took us straight to Mo's place.

Mo answered his door and invited us inside. He didn't offer us a chair but we each found a wall we could lean on while he talked.

"Stu is my neighbor," he began. "He owns the brownstone next door and lives in the downstairs level with his dog, 'Grrr.' He should have named him 'Bark' or 'Growl' or 'Ruff' because he barks all the time . . . at least when someone he doesn't know comes around. He even barks at me and I've known him for two years."

Mona and I both nodded our heads to let him know we were following his every word.

"On Halloween night . . . ," he paused. "Uh, Mike? . . . Who's the girl?"

He reached out his hand to Mona, she reached back and they gave each other a little shake.

"I'm Moe and you are . . . ?"

To my horror Mona got "that" look in her eyes and said, "I'm Mona. I am one of the people on Mr. Maurison's staff at the agency. He does the work and I do the step and fetching."

Moe looked impressed.

"Good going, Mike. I had no idea I was hiring a big shot detective."

"Neither did I," I said. "But you were saying something about Halloween . . . ."

"Yeah, okay . . . right . . . On Halloween the dog was barking like mad. Believe it or not we actually get some kids coming around here trick or treating. They come early, before it gets dark, and visit buildings where they

109

know people. Most families know Stu because whenever he takes the dog for a walk the kids gravitate to him as if he was a black hole. Kids love dogs even though Grrr would just as soon bite their hands off when they try to pet him. So that's why they kept showing up at Stu's place and that's why the dog kept barking until it got dark.

"Stu told me that around 7:00 p.m. he left the dog locked in his apartment while he went out for dinner. When he got back, his place was empty except for the dog. The back door had been forced open so he took a look around to see if anything was missing. Whoever had come in seemed to have left empty-handed so he didn't call the cops.

"The next morning he came over to my place to ask if I saw or heard anything suspicious between 7:00-8:30 the night before. Since I'd been reading, I hadn't been looking out the windows so I hadn't seen anything and I hadn't heard anything either. With the kids gone, the whole neighborhood was like 'Silent Night, Holy Night' but without the baby Jesus. There's more to the story but let's go next door and I'll let Stu tell you the rest."

As we went up the steps to Stu's front door, we heard a dog beginning to bark incessantly as though he could smell us coming a mile away. Like I said, dogs like me enough to eat me so I let Mo and Mona do the honors of knocking on the door.

Stu turned out to be an older gentleman who, if what Mo had told us was true, must have been more well-off than fifteen or twenty of me would be. Owning a brownstone in Manhattan like Stu apparently did, would give him a nest egg of $2-3 million or more, especially in

110

a nice neighborhood like this one. As we went inside Stu held Grrr on a leash, keeping him from attacking us.

"Oh, don't worry about Grrr," he said. "Once he sees I'm not threatened by you he'll calm down. He pays for his keep since with him around I have never felt the need to invest in a security alarm system. That's why the person who broke in didn't trigger any sirens or bells. And that's why I can't figure out why Grrr let me down. He is getting older and I suppose if he was asleep in the basement he might have missed it but . . . ."

"Oh dear, excuse me," he said, interrupting himself. "You must be the private investigator Mo told me about."

"Mike Maurison," I replied. "A pleasure to meet you, Mr. . . . ."

"Moshowitz, Stu Moshowitz." Turning to Mona he added, "And this is . . . ?"

"This is Mona, my assistant" I said with a wink in her direction."

Stu then introduced us to three men he had invited over to play bridge that evening. Michel had been his partner when they had run a law firm together and was an amateur archaeologist. Gordon was a dog breeder who, over the years, had given both Grrr and his predecessor to Stu as friendship gifts. He had also been Stu's investment broker for over twenty years. Last, but not least, was Marty, a retired surgeon and naval officer who Stu had met at the Metropolitan Club where they were both members. Marty was also an art collector who currently had a painting on loan to the Metropolitan Museum of Art: a small Renoir pastel sketch of a young female bather I had seen some weeks before. I wanted to talk art with him but I was there on business so I forced myself to reassert my professional persona.

"So what's the deal," I began. "Mo tells me nothing was taken so why am I here?"

"Something was taken," Stu replied, "but I didn't discover it until two days ago. The whole thing is a little dicey so I am hoping you will be discreet."

"My ears are on auto-pilot but my mouth doesn't work unless I tell it to," I said. "Go ahead. It sounds like it's going to be a good story."

"Well, at least it is a short one. You see, like my friends here I enjoy collecting things. But unlike my friends I prefer to collect small things like Chinese snuff boxes, European miniatures and cameos from just about everywhere. I also have one of the largest collections of Tiffany earrings outside of Tiffany's own collection. The items I don't put in my safe deposit box I keep in a secure safe in a place that, for obvious reasons, I'm not going to reveal to you.

"Lately, though, I have become interested in Middle Eastern artifacts. I even wound up buying one that had been stolen from the Bagdad Museum and smuggled out of Iraq during the war. Of course I returned it as soon as I found it out. But back to the story: There are a lot of artifacts that are dug up or picked up by scavengers in places like Israel, Syria, Jordan, and, of course, Iraq, Afghanistan and, well, places like that. It's not exactly illegal to own these things but it is illegal to take them out of the countries where they were found. Because the original, precise location where they were found is not recorded, they are called "unprovenanced" which lowers their archaeological value but not necessarily their value for collectors.

"I recently acquired a small seal that had likely been found in Israel, probably from somewhere near Jerusalem. A seal, by the way, is like a signet ring, used to press the owner's name into soft wax or clay. Seals were used in correspondence, as a mark of ownership, and as a means of securing something, like the seal on Jesus' tomb. The clay impression is called a bulla and I have collected a number of those as well.

"From what Michel and those more versed in such things have told me, my seal is what is called a" LMLK" seal from the 8th century BC. These royal seals are associated with the reign of the biblical Israelite King Hezekiah. Thousands of clay jar handles and other clay fragments have been found with seal impressions on them very similar to mine. But this would be the very first actual seal ever recovered. If it isn't a forgery it is beyond priceless. Even without provenance, it would be considered a treasure . . . even by most of the archaeological community who generally despise and shun such illegally-acquired artifacts."

"So," I said. "This is what has gone missing?"

"Yes. I have many trusted friends who could verify I had possession of the seal. But I have enjoyed looking at it, holding it and studying it so much I haven't been putting it back in the safe as often as I should. Halloween night was one of those nights. When I went out to dinner, I set it down on that bookshelf over there in the corner. As you can see there are a good number of artifacts, all of minimal value, that I keep there for visitors to look at.

"Coming home I forgot about it until yesterday when, after I remembered where I had placed it, I discovered it was gone. The burglar must have taken it. Either they knew what they were looking for or else they were the damndest and luckiest thief in history. So you see the problem I have. I can't report it to the police because I could get into trouble as a collector and, even if they found it, the seal would be repatriated to Israel. I can't report it to my insurance company for the same reasons. So I have lost the seal and the considerable amount of money I paid for it. I'm hoping that somehow you can help me catch the thief or find the seal. I really can't imagine you having any success in this but I would be grateful if you would try."

"I'm not sure I can be of any help," I said. "There's so little to go on. It happened too long ago to collect any fingerprints that might have been left and I don't know enough about the antiquities market to find out if it has shown up somewhere. I'm sure you, Michel and a thousand other people would have a better chance of finding it than I have."

Mona sidled up next to me and said, "Come over here with me for a moment. Your assistant has something she'd like to say to you."

Once we were out of earshot from the others she said, "What sort of detective are you? Gordon's got the seal and you might as well get this whole thing over with so we can go home."

Mona had left me speechless.

"Uh, . . . what did I miss?" I stammered.

"What you missed is a piece of literature you should have remembered. Here, let me refresh your memory:

Arthur Conan Doyle . . . *Silver Blaze* . . . Now do you get it?"

I had to think way back to my childhood to remember how Sherlock Holmes solved that mystery; whatever it was; I couldn't remember what it was. Was it a murder? No, it wasn't a murder. The story had to do with a horse and . . . wait . . . there was "the curious incident of the dog in the night-time." Hmmm . . . and what do dogs do? Dogs smell and bark and . . . and then I remembered.

Holmes figured out "whodunit" because the dog didn't bark. Just like Grrr hadn't barked. Who else in the world, besides Stu, would Grrr have known well enough not to have barked at? That could only be the man who had raised him from a pup. And that would be Gordon, who not only knew the dog but also knew about the seal.

I nudged Mona on the arm and said, "Well done, Watson."

When confronted, Gordon tearfully confessed to having coveted the seal from the first time he had seen it. An irrepressible passion had grown into uncontrollable greed. He was ashamed of what he had done. He had the seal tucked away in his sock drawer and felt as though the weight of the world would fall from his shoulders if he could return it.

I'm not too sure what happened after that but I suspect Stu found himself a new investment broker. As for Mona and me, I took the generous reward Stu paid me for the part I played in solving the case. I then split it 50-50 with Mona. If pride goeth before a fall then I needed Mona to scrape me off the floor and give mouth-to-mouth resuscitation to help me re-inflate my ego. To her credit she has never rubbed it in. Who says a degree in English Literature isn't worth anything these days?

The next day was Tuesday.

One thing I don't do as a private eye is take cases that involve drugs. It doesn't mean I won't take a case that involves someone who is *on* drugs—if I did that I would have to turn down nearly half of the cases I work on each year. But when it comes to drug dealers I'd rather let someone else handle the job. It's one of those things where I choose to value my own life more than I value trying to bust some drug-running sleaze-bag and get him thrown into jail. Even so, in spite of all my precautions, every once in a while I find myself in a situation that, like the plague, I should have been able to avoid.

On Tuesday afternoon I was hired by a man around forty years old who was worried about his sixteen year old daughter. She had gotten into the routine of leaving the house two or three nights a week with a group of people she said were her friends. She'd get home at midnight, one o'clock a.m. or later. Weekends or school nights—it didn't matter. Her grades had gone down like the Titanic and her parents couldn't figure out a way to assert control short of giving her up to foster care. The daughter, whose name was Stacie, would yell at them if or whenever they tried to rein her in.

"You can't do anything to me," she'd say. "Go ahead. Try beating me or try locking me in my closet. I'll call the cops and you'll both do jail time. Is that what you want? Does that sound fun to you? So just leave me alone. I'm sixteen and I am old enough to live my life the way I want. Just butt out and leave me alone."

Somehow, Stacie was missing the irony in all that. After all, her parents were providing her with a home, a warm room, a bed, food on the table and more in the fridge. Not to mention health insurance, clothes, a computer, an iPhone and lots of other things teenagers take for granted—as though it was their unalienable right to have them.

The whole thing reminded me of a book I came across while browsing at the bookstore where Mona works. It's title was, *Get Out Of My Life, But First Could You Drive Me and Cheryl To The Mall?: A Parent's Guide to the New Teenager*. I didn't read the book but the title seemed to catch the gist of what the guy was trying to tell me about his daughter. I suggested that he check out the book and I said it for no good reason other than I thought the title was so awesome. He was so desperate he actually wrote down the suggestion of a thirty year-old single male who hadn't talked to a teenager since he turned twenty.

The man wanted me to follow his daughter to see where she went and to try and find out as much as I could about her so-called "friends." For him it was a last-chance effort to save his daughter from self-destructing like one of those reel-to-reel tapes at the beginning of the TV version of *Mission Impossible*. Business had been both slow and boring for me lately so I said "Yes" even though my guts felt a little unsure about the whole thing. I deluded myself into thinking it was indigestion and jumped into what turned out to be an abyss.

The whole scenario seemed very unclear to me. On the one hand, the daughter could simply be going to karaoke bars and singing golden oldies with her friends until her voice gave out. On the other hand, she could be raising money for her friends by taking walks up and down a sidewalk somewhere or she could be spending her evenings getting strung out on pot, ecstasy or oxycodone. If I had been thinking more clearly I might have considered the possibility of saying, "No thank you. Why don't you find someone who already has an albatross hanging around their neck?" or something to that effect.

But I didn't. And that was why I found myself on East 66th Street at 7:00 p.m. the following evening sitting in my friend Sid's car waiting for someone else's car to pull up in front of Stacie's apartment. It didn't help that the city was doing repairs that narrowed the street to one lane. A red-curbed loading zone served my needs until Stacie's friends showed up in an SUV at 7:15. After she climbed in, the car went towards Central Park with me trying to keep it in sight through the early November darkness. One nice benefit of living in the City is that, even at night, there is so much light on the main streets it's not much different from driving at midday. After we turned left on Park Avenue I got close enough to jot down the license plate info along with the make and model of the car. The car travelled all the way south to Union Square where Park Avenue ends and then made a right on 14th. After a few more minutes, the car pulled into a small public garage in the area where the Village, Chelsea and the Meatpacking District converge—all three once rated among the five "least safe" areas in Manhattan. I had put my .380 in the glove compartment just in case and it looked as though this might just be the case. Since there was no place else to park the car I followed them into the garage, took my ticket and found a place about fifteen stalls down from theirs. I slid the pistol into my shoulder holster and waited until they got out of their car and started walking. Then I got out and followed from what traditionally is called a "discrete distance."

They walked to a door and stood there a moment. Then the door opened, they walked through and the door closed. The door turned out to be a security door that required a resident card to unlock it.

With no way to go in, I walked out the exit from the garage and looked up at the six story apartment building that stood on top of it. Somewhere inside that building, Stacie and her friends were doing something. Nearby I could see several banks, a delicatessen and a coffee shop along with a wide mix of chain and independent retail businesses. A busy subway stop was just down the street. If this was a high crime area then the bad guys must have all been hiding in back alleys or beating each other up behind closed doors. I certainly didn't see any of them walking down the street. I felt embarrassed by the lump under my left arm and I couldn't see any reason for wearing it, at least not in this neighborhood. After a minute or two, I decided I didn't want to miss the kids if they left early so I went back to my car, slid the .380 back into the glove compartment and settled in for what I figured would be a long evening. I didn't want to drink coffee because I had nowhere to pee except into a can. So lately I've been trying out those pills that advertize five hours of energy. I haven't figured out whether they actually work or not but they sure don't taste as good as hot caffeine in a cup.

At exactly midnight, the door opened and out came the same four kids who had gone in over four hours earlier. I followed them back to Stacie's apartment where

119

she got out, no doubt anticipating another argument with her anxious parents. I stayed in the hunt and followed the SUV until it dropped the other two passengers off at the corner of Lexington and East 99th. After an illegal u-turn on Lexington I followed the driver back to a private underground parking garage near York and East 89th.just a block or so from the East River. A check on the car registration gave me the name Maurice Collier and an address on East 89th. I wasn't about to close out the case but I was one or two steps closer.

Bright and early the next morning, which for me was around 10:00 a.m., I walked over to the police station on East 67th to have a check run on Mr. Collier. Maurice turned out to be thirty-seven years old with one conviction, one suspended sentence for possession of a controlled substance twelve years ago, and clean since. I figured the youngster driving his car was either his son or someone else close enough to be trusted with Collier's $35,000 SUV.

With that info under my belt it didn't take me long to discover Collier was married to Mina and had two children, Maureen, 19 and Mitchell, 18. Mitchell had both a driver's license and a fairly impressive rap sheet for a young man his age. Since he turned 13, he had faced juvenile charges of violent assault, firearm possession, resisting arrest, public intoxication, possession of stolen property and—like father like son—possession of a controlled substance. Mitch didn't seem to have had done too well with first chances but when it came to second chances he was up there with the best. Except for a month in juvenile detention he had been let go every time.

I had a funny feeling Stacie's father was not going to be favorably impressed when I gave him a description of his daughter's new friend.

Mitchell had dropped out of high school his sophomore year and, so far as I could tell, hadn't had a job or done anything else since. He seemed to enjoy a fairly good life-style given the clothes and jewelry he was wearing when I had seen him the previous evening. Since he seemed to be the man in charge, I decided to invest my time in following him around for a few days.

Mitch turned out to be an active guy and not the sort who chooses a couch potato to be his" mini wii" alter-ego. On Friday morning he left his apartment building at 9:30 a.m. and walked to the nearest bus stop. He caught the #31 bus to 9th Avenue, switched to the #11 and went directly south through Chelsea to 14th Street where he got off. He then walked one block over to the same apartment building he had driven to on Wednesday night. After two or three hours he put himself into reverse and headed back home. He holed up in his own apartment for the rest of the day until 7:00 p.m. when he pulled out of his garage in the SUV, picked up two young men at Lexington and East 99th, picked up Stacie at 7:15 and did a repeat of what they'd done the night before, almost to the minute.

Tailing someone is an art similar to walking on a tightrope. One slip and you're toast. Normally it is done from a distance where the suspect won't ever see you. But this almost always means you miss important details such as who they're meeting with in a restaurant or what they're doing in a riverfront warehouse. The rule of thumb is that you can only expose yourself once. Try it twice and you put yourself at risk of being recognized. So this is how I planned out my surveillance. On Friday morning I had gotten lucky by tracking Mitch's bus rides in my friend's car. This is the safest way to follow but it is always easy to lose the guy in a crowd or when they get on or off a bus. Traffic patterns and even the badly-timed arrival of a large truck can mess things up. Worse than that, if the person you are following disappears into a subway station you are pretty much done for the rest of the day.

On Saturday morning, I took Zach, my friend Thor's nephew, along for the ride. After watching Mitch walk to the bus stop from his apartment, I drove straight down through Chelsea and parked in the now-familiar garage fifteen minutes before the bus was scheduled to drop him off at 14th. When I saw two men drive into the garage, park their car and walk over to the security door Zach and I ambled over and pretended to fumble in our pockets for something. When they opened the door, I said, "Hey, thanks," and started to follow them inside. But one of the men turned and said, "Get outta here. Open the door with your own card."

A young couple with their arms full of groceries came along a couple of minutes later. This time I offered to hold the door open for them when they went in. They not only didn't object to our following them in but they even said "Thank you." I went up to the sixth floor and found a chair to sit in next to the elevator. Zach did the same on the first floor above the garage. The next time the elevator started up from the garage Zach pushed the "up" button and when the elevator stopped, he got on. Mitch was in the elevator so Zach punched the button that was already lit. So he and Mitch got off on the fifth floor together where Zach could see him knock on the door of #513 and go inside.

After coming up to the sixth floor, Zach gave me his report and I sent him back down to attach a small micro-amplification/transmitter device under the doorknob where it would be as inconspicuous as possible. It was a new toy I had recently purchased over the internet and I was interested to see how well it worked. Zach asked if it this was legal and I told him no, it wasn't. But since I wasn't going to use it as evidence in a criminal prosecution no one would know and no one would care except for the bad guys and they would only draw attention to themselves if they made a stink about it.

"Don't sweat it. It'll be just fine," I said with as much sincerity as I could fake.

While he went downstairs, I got to thinking maybe this wasn't such a good idea after all. There was also the small matter of trespassing on private property in a secured area but, in this case, we hadn't forced our way or misrepresented ourselves to get in. It might be a stretch but, after all, we had freely and publicly been allowed entry by residents of the building. The law is drawn up like a fine line and sometimes it's hard to know what side of the line you should straddle.

Once Zach got the device in place, I began taping whatever there was to record, which wasn't much. Just conversation about some girls and a trip to Texas one of them was planning. It was clear they were busy doing something the whole time but I couldn't tell what it was.

After an hour or so I started to get a little nervous about the time. I wanted to clear out before Mitchell came out of the room. So I asked Zach to go back down, retrieve my stuff from the door and meet me back at the car.

He said, "No. I'm not going back down there. This whole thing is starting to scare me. You do it and I'll meet *you* back at the car."

It made sense that I shouldn't send someone to do a job I wasn't willing to do myself. But the whole point was so I wouldn't blow my cover. I didn't really have much choice, though, because I couldn't leave the building with the listening device left on the door. So we went down to the fifth floor together, I handed Zach the tape and my car keys, I got off and Zach went down to my car.

As the elevator doors closed, I whispered a final thought, "If something happens call the cops, okay?"

The doors closed but I added one more thought to no one in particular, "Seriously—call the cops!"

In a casual, sauntering sort of way I went down the hall to # 513. It would only take me one second to pull the device off, turn around and make my way back to the elevator. When I got about ten feet from the door another door opened at the end of the hall. A nondescript man in his early twenties stepped out of the exit stairway and started down the hall in my direction.

Sheez, what bad timing, was all I could think. *What do I do now?*

I figured I would keep on walking and disappear into the door where the guy had just come out and then wait for him to go wherever he was going. After a minute or two, I'd come back out, do my thing and split.

I never made it to the door. In fact, I didn't even make it past the guy.

Right in front of room #513, he stepped in front of me, held up his hand and asked, "Are you looking for this?"

Before I could think of a witty comeback he sucker-punched me with his other hand. I went to my knees in a daze. The door opened, I saw Mitch standing there looking like someone who was swearing but I couldn't be sure because I couldn't hear anything and then everything disappeared into night.

When I came to, I was trussed up like a roast turkey with a blindfold over my eyes, duct tape over my mouth, a ringing in my ears, and a headache that was putting migraines to shame. I could hear several voices talking at the same time but, with the bells of St. Mary's ringing in my ears, it was hard for me to join in as part of the conversation.

"What the . . . are we supposed . . . dump body . . . take . . . will be pissed . . . alone . . . someone else with him . . . bad enough but . . . do it right . . . no one . . . ."

It was all interspersed with as much cussing and swearing as . . . well . . . as me hitting my finger with a hammer . . . but with a more extensive and flamboyant vocabulary.

I was surprisingly calm about it all—probably because there was nothing I could do except to lie on the floor like the lady in the TV ad who used to say. "I've fallen and I can't get up."

Out of habit I began trying to think of something that would change the odds back in my favor but after a minute or two I gave it up. With some relief, I remembered I had left my gun and wallet in the car and— Zach! I had completely forgotten about Zach.

Please God, I prayed. *Make Zach call the police! Please!*

I started to add, *I'll do anything . . . I'll even start going to church!* but I had already been invited to go to church with Mona and had turned it down . . . Mona! . . . I had completely forgotten about Mona, too!

Oh, God! Get me out of this mess because of Mona!

I wasn't sure what I meant by it but I let it go and left it for God figure out.

Then suddenly and without any advance notice, my head twisted violently and smashed into the wall. I was out so fast I doubt if I even twitched.

I came to for a second time, this time with the sounds of Manhattan all around me accompanied by a symphony of sirens. I was still half awake and half asleep when, as though floating in a dream, I was wheeled out of the ambulance and rolled into the St. Luke's ER. I heard the words "x-ray" and "skull fracture" and decided I would go back to sleep.

It turned out my prayers were answered after all. Zach had waited in the car for fifteen minutes; long enough for him to wish he had a bed nearby he could crawl under. In spite of feeling as though he might need to change his pants in a few minutes he had the presence of mind to call 911. Although Zach's father is from Vietnam Zach has never spoken anything but English since he was born . . . except sometimes at home when he's trying to explain something to his father's aunt who lives with them. He was suitably baffled when he heard himself speaking to the 911 operator in Vietnamese. She had already signaled to her supervisor that she needed a translator when Zach got his train back on the tracks and started over again. To his surprise and relief, in less than ten minutes three police cars pulled into the garage one after the other. After he finished explaining the situation, they forcibly opened the security door. Two cops went up the elevator, two went up the stairs and two stayed down in the garage with Zach.

Apparently, from what I was told, they quietly approached apartment #513, stood carefully on both sides of the door, knocked loudly and shouted, "Police! Open the door and come out with your hands up."

Or something like that.

And like good boy scouts the three guys inside did a good turn and came out of the room just like they had been told by the nice men with the badges and guns.

When the cops looked inside they saw two things in the following order. First they saw a meth lab with equipment, tables and chemicals taking up most of the floor space in the two-bedroom apartment. The second thing they saw was me, lying deathly still on the floor under a state-of-the-art ventilation system with blood oozing out of my right ear.

Stacie's parents got a lot more than they had bargained for and so did I. I spent six days in the hospital and got paid $500 for my trouble. If there was any upside to the fiasco it was that Mitch and his friends ran out of second chances and, after having her felony reduced to a misdemeanor, Stacie was sent home to her parents a little sadder, a little wiser, and a little more humble than before.

The upside for me was that I got to see more of Mona. She came every evening after work and spent most of her days off keeping me company. We talked about art and philosophy and our childhood. We talked about hopes and dreams and . . . well, we talked about everything in the world . . . except about us. I think each of us had the feeling something was changing in our relationship. For me at least, it felt like the equivalent of giving Mona a fraternity pin. I don't really know how she felt about it because, as I already said, we didn't talk about it.

In spite of the prayers and promises I made while lying on the apartment floor I didn't start going to church with Mona and I didn't fall into bed with God, either. But, just like something had changed between me and Mona, something had changed between me and God, too. For the first time in my life, I had found someone to say "Thank you" to for everything and for nothing in particular. It also crossed my mind that the odds had inexplicitly shifted in my favor and that, for some reason I did not completely understand, I had been given a second chance.

Chapter 8

More than Chestnuts
December

Mid-December in New York City: The Promethean Tree and ice skating rink in Rockefeller Center, the Christmas decorations at Macy*s and FAO Schwartz, the pleasant, random surprise of warm air rising from sidewalk vents, the sound of Salvation Army bell ringers and brass players, assorted street carolers and, of course, the Santas "Ho-Ho-Ho-ing" everywhere you turn.

Not to mention the slippery slush, the bone-chilling, humid winter air and the densely-packed crowds of shoppers and gawkers pushing their way through equally dense crowds of ordinary people simply trying, like spawning salmon, to swim against the current on their way to work somewhere in the City.

It was a Wednesday morning and I was one of those poor, red-from-the cold, hunchbacked salmon pushing my way through the crushing sweat of multitudes of bundled men, women and children, trying to reach the spawning ground where I had an appointment with a new client who said his name was "Richard Dreyfuss-not-the-actor." I'm no actor, either, and I'm not really a salmon. I'm just Mike Maurison, Private Eye, trying to earn a day's pay in the winter wonderland of Manhattan.

Actually, unlike most people around here I don't mind the cold and the slush. That's just part of the natural order of things and I couldn't change any of it even if I wanted to. It's Christmas I can't stand; Christmas and all the trimmings that go along with it. My name might be Mike Maurison but when December comes around each year, my middle name is Scrooge. Not the Disney version but the mean, yell-at-the-children, tightwad, skinflint, hard as nails, cold as ice, don't give a damn, Dicken's character. Bah and Humbug. Go ahead and buy a turkey. Buy the biggest and the best turkey you can find. Buy the prize-winning turkey if you really want to. Here's a shilling. Take it and go away. And don't bother to come back. Beat it and get lost.

If it wasn't for Christmas, I might actually enjoy December in Manhattan.

Call it sour grapes. Or call it a neurosis stemming from my childhood. I grew up without a mother, and my father was too busy working to even bother to set up decorations around the house. When Christmas Day finally rolled around, he managed to pull a beat-up artificial tree out of a battered box and throw some tangled tinsel on it. Some years he would use an extension cord and somehow manage to clip a light bulb onto the top of the tree as if it was a star. For him it seemed more like a chore than a pleasure. For me there was no magic in it at all and when I watched *White*

Christmas, It's a Wonderful Life and *Miracle on 34th Street* on the TV I would laugh all the way through them as though they were old Laurel and Hardy movies.

I did get presents. Usually new socks, underwear and, every year without fail, a small balsa glider and an orange in my stocking which I hung on the knob of one of the dresser drawers in my bedroom . . . because, well, because my father said it was what kids did on Christmas Eve.

I never believed in Santa, either. That may have been because my father had no one to watch me when he went shopping so he always took me along. He didn't even have me close my eyes when he bought the socks, the underwear and the orange. Don't get me wrong. My father was a good man and I loved him until he died. But Christmas was depressing even back then and it hasn't gotten any better now that I am thirty.

Dreyfuss wanted me to meet him in his office. I figured he must be someone important because the address he gave me was on an upper floor of 30 Rockefeller Plaza, high above NBC Studio H-8 where I had once been given a ticket to see *Saturday Night Live* being taped. A secretary greeted me with a friendly smile and asked me to make myself comfortable while she confirmed my appointment. Less than a minute later, she ushered me into a luxury office with a million-dollar view across the East River.

The cost of the man's business suit would have more than paid the next month's rent for my apartment and office space combined. He didn't stand up but he did point me to a chair in front of his polished rosewood desk.

"I don't have a lot of time to spend on this," he began. "What did you say your name was, again?"

"Mike Maurison," I replied in the deepest, most resonant voice I could muster.

"And you are a private eye, a detective of some sort?"

"Yes, sir, I am."

I wasn't usually this formal but, to be honest the whole set-up was a bit intimidating for a guy who eats at corner diners and works in a dingy office with a pressboard desk.

"And you're good at this?"

"Yes sir," I repeated. "I like to think that I am."

"Then I will give you a chance to prove it to me. Here's the deal. There's someone I play golf with named Ben Styler. I think he's been ripping me off. Not on the golf course, I mean. We only play twenty-dollars a hole so that doesn't add up to much and none of us cheats, at least so far as I can tell.

"Ben is my lawyer and handles my financial affairs: investments, properties, insurance; those sorts of things. I think he's done a good job and I trust him with all of this. If I didn't, I'd get him thrown out of the country club and would dump him as my attorney.

"Here's the problem. He is also the lawyer for my daughter, Becky. It's her I'm worried about. She says he is charging her fees that seem too high and her investments haven't been doing as well as mine have been lately. Not that anyone's investments have been doing very well but you get the idea.

"I want you to look into this and see if you can find anything that seems out of sorts. My daughter doesn't seem to want to tell me more than she already has but she did say she would talk to someone like you who could keep things confidential and below the radar if you know what I mean."

Dreyfuss had shoveled a truckload of information into my brain and I was having trouble chewing on it enough to swallow any of it. But I did hear the word "daughter" and the phrase "someone like you" and the thought of what these people might be willing to pay me kept me chewing as hard and as fast as I could.

As if he was reading my mind, he continued by saying, "I'll be willing to pay you whatever your standard fee is plus ten percent along with any expenses. Is that all right with you? Do you want a written contract or are you willing to take my offer with a handshake?"

"A handshake is as good as gold to me," I said, although with anybody else an offer like that would have seemed more like gold-plate over base-metal.

He reached across his desk, looked me straight in the eyes and grabbed my hand with a tight squeeze. I got the impression he was making it clear I had better meet his expectations or he would pressure my landlord to revoke my office lease. That didn't frighten me but it did quicken my resolve to make this case a priority.

He pushed a buzzer on his phone. His secretary came in and ushered me out of the office. I could see him punching the buttons on his phone as the door closed behind me.

The secretary gave me what I needed to know: Becky's home address and phone number, Ben's home and office information and a reminder to make a professional contact with Becky by tomorrow afternoon at the latest.

I pulled out my business card but she handed it back saying, "That's not necessary. We already have all the information about you we need including your Social Security number, your driver's license number, two or three reference interviews with former clients and a list of every parking ticket and moving violation you have ever had."

I was impressed but it crossed my mind that if they could find out all that stuff about me why did they need me to figure out what Ben Styler was up to?

I didn't share my thoughts out loud but I did try to make a joke by saying, "After all this you were willing to hire me anyway?"

She didn't laugh or even smile.

She just pointed me towards the door and said, "Good day and good luck."

I went back to my dingy office with the fifteen-dollar view and wrote up a report on a stake-out I had done for a shop owner whose store kept getting tagged by some wanna-be street artist. Graffiti has its place, I guess, just as long as it's not sprayed on my place. Last night the kid came by, painted a fresco and walked six buildings down the road where he went in the front door. I took down the address and put it down in my report. I planned to give it to the shopkeeper tomorrow along with a clear infrared photo I took of Mr. Michelangelo Jr. Then I'd let him take it from there. If there was a hearing or a trial I'd be the star witness and pick up some more spare change for my trouble.

With that out of the way I had a clear shot at my new priority case. I pulled out my cell phone and called Becky.

A woman's voice with a foreign accent I couldn't place answered the phone saying, "Hello?"

Not very creative but I guess it was enough to get a conversation going.

"My name is Mike Maurison. I believe that Ms. Dreyfuss is expecting my call."

"Ms. Who?" came the reply.

"Uh, how about Ms. Becky?"

"Oh, you mean Mrs. Brunhoff. If you'll hold for a minute I'll tell her you are on the line."

There followed one those long silences when you are glad there isn't an audio tape full of elevator music droning into your ear while you wait.

I had only counted to one hundred and twelve when I heard another, "Hello?" but this time with a different female voice behind it.

"Is this Becky Brunhoff?" I asked.

"Yes. Are you the man my father said would be calling me about . . . well . . . about something where I need some help and advice?"

"That would be me. Mike Maurison, Private Investigator."

I prefer this particular title over "Private Eye" when talking with a potential client who has lots of dough because it sounds more sophisticated.

"Maybe," I continued, "we should get together and talk. What would be a good time for you?"

"Oh, we don't have to meet. I can tell you everything over the phone right now if you'd like."

I didn't know what to say so I shuffled around in my desk drawer looking for a pencil and note pad. When I was ready to jot stuff down I said, "Sure, why not. Let's give it a shot."

"No, no!" came the reply in a voice half an octave higher than it had been before. "I don't want you to shoot anybody. Please. That's not the sort of help I need. What I want you to do is follow my husband and see where he goes on Thursday evenings. He says he is going to a weekly board meeting for some sort of charitable organization he is a trustee for. But no meeting should be going on so long that he can't make it back home before 12:30 or 1:30 in the morning. When I ask about it he just says he goes out for a cup of decaf coffee afterwards to tie up the loose ends with some of the other trustees."

She paused as though giving time for it to sink in. As for me, it wasn't what I was expecting to hear but it was straight forward enough so that I didn't need to waste any pencil lead on it.

To let her know I was still alive and listening I said, "Okay, forget the gun thing. I am hearing you have some doubt as to the veracity of your husband's explanation?"

"If you mean I don't believe him? Well, then you'd be right. It's gets a bit more convoluted because one of the other so-called trustees is Ben Styler. He's my father's lawyer and my financial advisor. I called his wife a few days ago to ask her what she thought of this. She says she's having the same problem with Ben. He tells her he is going to these meetings and comes home late, too, with the same excuse about the decaf coffee.

"I want you to check this out but I don't want my father to know anything about it. Sometimes, well, all too often, he sticks his nose into other people's business in a well-meaning, meddling, suffocating, controlling sort of way if you know what I mean. So please leave him out of this. I am the one who is hiring you even though my father probably told you otherwise. Whatever my father said he'd pay you I'll match it. Okay?"

This was getting complicated and my head was running out of room to store all the data the dame was downloading.

"That's fine with me but, since we can't shake hands on it at the moment I'd like to have it in writing, including the bit about my fees plus ten-percent and expenses. I'll start the case right away but if I don't get a certified letter from you in two days I'll drop it like an over-broiled tomato."

"Fine," she said. "I'll do it. But write this down: My husband's name is Matthew Brunhoff. He doesn't like to be called Matt. I think you already have my address. He leaves the house at 6:30 p.m. on Thursdays in his 2015 black Lexus. It's a hybrid. I think it says "GS" on the back end. I don't remember what the license number is but you should be able to figure that out if you're any good at what you do. I have no idea where he goes for these meetings or even what the name of the charity is. That's it. Do you have any questions? I don't expect you to figure it out in just one week but I am hoping that after two Thursdays you be able to give a report that will satisfy me."

"I'll do my best. That's all I can promise. But, one more thing: Your father said something about your having a concern about the way Styler is handling your finances. What's with that?"

"I have some concerns about that. I really do. But I made it a bigger deal with my father just to throw him off from what's really worrying me about my husband."

So far as I knew I had all the info I needed so I said, "I'll be in touch" and she said "Good-bye" and "Thank you" and the conversation was over.

There was nothing left on my calendar so I called Mona.

If I had anything to say about it I would not have chosen the name "Mona" for my girlfriend. To me it sounds too much like "moan" and "groan" and as a result it isn't the sort of name that perks up my spirits on a bleak, mid-December, Manhattan afternoon. But she is the best friend I have ever had and we have spent a lot of time together since we met back in September. It turned out that since she was free for dinner that night I now had something to put in the blank space in my date book.

We ate at a place that was not particularly elegant but was at least warmer than the air outside. Mona talked and talked about Christmas and repeated her invitation for me to spend the day with her and her family in Jersey. As you might guess the thought of spending Christmas Day with a large group of happy, cheerful people did not particularly inspire me to say, "Yes."

So I said, "Sounds good to me but I'll have to see what my schedule's going to be. You never can tell in my business."

She also invited me to a Christmas Eve service at her church on Fifth Avenue.

I asked if there would be any music and she said, "Of course, silly! There's always music at a Christmas Eve service."

I figured that if I went, there would be a crowd and I wouldn't have to talk to anyone or to pretend I was happy to be there. If I treated it like a concert at Carnegie Hall, I supposed I could get through it as a favor to Mona.

So I said, "Sure. I can do that."

The next day was Thursday. I dropped off the info on the graffiti case at my client's shop, made some phone calls, had a long lunch at a local pizza place and made another phone call, this time to my friend, Sid, to ask if I could borrow his car for the night. If you know anything about Manhattan you will know you have to be a millionaire to own a car. Well, maybe not a millionaire, but you have to be more rich or famous than I am to be able to afford one. So I walk a lot or take the bus, the subway or maybe a cab or a rental car when I can afford it or when my job requires it. Since I get paid for expenses it usually comes out even anyway.

Sid isn't rich or famous either, but because of his job he gets a free parking place not too far from his apartment. Since he lives so close to where he works the car sits there most of the time gathering dust. When I need a car for a stakeout or to tail someone Sid usually lets me borrow it. It's not completely out of the goodness of his heart, of course. That's as rare a thing to find in NYC as it is to find a taxi when it's raining and you really need one in a hurry. Sid lets me borrow his car because he owes me big time for helping him reverse a child-custody case he lost to the mother of his two kids. I got the dirt on his ex-wife and he got the kids. He couldn't afford to pay me at the time so I get to drive his car when it is mutually convenient. In return, I fill the tank whether I used it up or not. I also keep his car key in my pocket in case of an emergency.

Sid said it would be okay so I picked up the car at 3:00 p.m. and started driving to Becky's place in Runson, New Jersey. If it was late at night I could make the trip one-way in about an hour and a half. But this would be the afternoon rush hour and I figured I needed a lot of slack to get there before 6:30 rolled around. Runson is a pretty classy area. Queen Latifah, Heather Locklear and Cher have all called it home at one time or another. It didn't surprise me when I heard that big-shot Richard Dreyfuss-not-the-actor's daughter lived there, too.

Traffic out of Manhattan wasn't too bad but the I-95 corridor through Newark was backed up from an overturned truck that had spilled a load of yellow rubber duckies all over the freeway . . . Really.

From Perth Amboy on it was clear sailing and I pulled into Rumson with forty-five minutes to spare. I drove by Becky's place to scope out a good place to park and did the drive-thru thing at a nearby McDonalds for a Big Mac combo, a cup of coffee and two pies for a dollar to hold me over for the rest of the night. Cold fries at 1 a.m. in the morning isn't much to look forward to but when a man is hungry it's any port in a storm.

At 6:00, I parked under a leafless elm tree one house down and across the street, pointing in the direction I guessed Matthew Brunhoff was going to go. I turned out to be right. At 6:30 sharp, the garage door opened and, even in the dark, the streetlight and the security lights that flashed on in front of the house were enough to show it was a black Lexus. I pulled out as he went past and at the first red light I wrote down the license number and noted a dent in the rear bumper that might be good to know if I had to ID the car from a distance.

I soon discovered one reason Matthew was getting home so late on Friday mornings. This was because I had the pleasure of driving behind him for an hour-and-a-half to Egg Harbor, just north of Ocean City with its famous Boardwalk. Ocean City might be a famous and popular summer destination but nobody goes there in the winter unless they have to; like because of a family emergency or an obligation that carries the threat of legal action if you turn it down.

The Lexus pulled into a Denny's parking lot. Matthew got out, walked over to a nearby dark-green Mercedes SUV, opened the passenger-side door and got in. The Mercedes lefy Denny's and drove straight into Ocean City proper where it pulled into a reasonably respectable motel. Matthew and the driver got out and the two men walked into the check-in area before entering an elevator to an upper floor without carrying a single piece of luggage or even a briefcase. My watch said 8:25 p.m. I left the engine idling to keep the heater going and resigned myself to several hours of trying to keep awake with the help of a disgusting pile of cold junk food and a cup of lukewarm caffeine.

I called a friend with the NYPD and gave him the license number on the SUV. In a few minutes, he called back and said it was registered in Middletown, New Jersey, to someone named Benjamin Styler.

The night was cold and clear and I was still wide awake when Ben and Matthew emerged from the elevator, waved at the desk clerk and got back into Ben's car. The return trip was the mirror image of the trip down and I had seen enough to write up a preliminary report for Becky in the morning. After putting Sids's car back where I found it, I walked into my flat and fell dead asleep onto my bed. My watch, if I had been conscious enough to look at it, said 2:30 a.m.

When I woke up, I was in the middle of a dream where I was in a big, crowded, Gothic-style church. Ben and Matthew were off to one side holding hands and Mona was up in the choir singing "Chestnuts Roasting on an Open Fire" like an angel. Most dreams disappear into the ether after a few minutes but this one somehow managed to etch itself into my memory like a key being dragged along a car door.

I decided I would call Becky and fill her in over the phone. I figured it would save me the time and trouble of having to write it all down. This time it was Becky's voice that said "Hello" at the other end.

"Hi, Becky. This is Mike Maurison. I thought you might like to hear what I came up with last night. Is it okay to talk about it on the phone? Is this a good time?"

"No one is here but me and the cat so you might as well tell me all about it."

I had the feeling Becky already knew what I was going to tell her and that the idea of using a gun had been floating around in her subconscious long before the subject came up during our first conversation. I also had the feeling she had hired me because she wanted to make sure her father wouldn't be involved and because she needed an independent, credible witness to confirm her suspicions.

I told her everything I had seen and done the night before with as much detail as I thought necessary. Becky listened quietly on the other end.

When I finished my narrative I said, "It's not my job to try and explain any of this and I don't have any idea what this might have to do with the money angle . . . ."

"It's alright," she interrupted. "I think I've got the picture now. I've always felt that Matthew was never completely happy in our marriage. We were more or less paired up by my father who knew Matthew's father at the country club. Of course he also knew Ben's father from the club, too. I guess I've lived in a bubble all my life. Maybe it's time for the bubble to pop."

It wasn't professional of me but I couldn't keep myself from saying, "I am so sorry to be the one who had to tell you this. I hope you'll be able to sort it out somehow and everything will work out for you. Let me know if there is anything else you would like me to do."

There was a pause and I started counting. I had only reached twenty-two when Becky answered by saying, "No. I think you have done everything that needs to be done, at least for the time being. I'll get back to you in a few days. In the meantime, I hope you will find time to enjoy the Christmas season with your friends and family."

As she finished it sounded like her voice began to choke up.

"Good-bye and thank you."

And she was gone.

That afternoon I received a certified and notarized letter from Becky that laid out the details of my contract. The following day, which was Saturday, I received another certified letter that contained a check for $5,000 made out to "Mike Maurison, Private Investigator." Along with the check was a short letter:

Dear Mr. Maurison,

Thank you for helping me face up to the sad reality of my relationship with Matthew. After my conversation with you, I phoned him at work and confronted him with what I knew about him and Ben. To my surprise he sounded almost relieved. He freely admitted he and Ben had fallen in love with each other and that they loved us both, too, and that they were very confused about how to work it out in a way that didn't devastate everybody involved. He also admitted he and Ben had been skimming some of my investment accounts by inflating fees and by withholding some dividends that should have been reinvested. He was very apologetic about this and said both he and Ben were ashamed to have allowed themselves to do such a horrible thing. He said he would be willing to cooperate on a divorce as long as Ben's name was left out of it and my father was completely cut out of the information loop. When the time came for Ben to get a divorce of his own then they would be willing to accept the consequences of their relationship and try to build a new life together as best they could.

I finished talking to him a few minutes ago and I want you to know I am alright with it. I haven't been happy in my relationship with Matthew for a whole lot of reasons, many of which revolve around my father. I have had a friend I have known from high

144

school who has been very supportive. He has never been married and has let me know that if my marriage to Matthew ever fell apart he would be happy to step in and love me and cherish me until the day we die.

Unless the divorce gets nasty for some reason, I believe my need for your services is over. I hope you have a Merry Christmas and I hope that I do, too.

Yours Sincerely,
Becky Brunhoff

And that was that.

After I cashed the check and paid some overdue bills my life went on as usual . . . until Christmas Eve finally came around.

It turned out to be one of those *déjà vu* moments when I saw the inside of Mona's church for the first time. It was exactly as it had been in my dream except that Ben and Matthew weren't there and Mona wasn't singing in the choir. No one sang the "chestnuts song," either, but the Christmas hymns and carols seemed to actually mean something to Mona and the people standing around us. The choir sang some music from Handel's *Messiah* and, for the first time in my life, I considered the possibility that the oratorio might be more than merely a representative example of beautiful music from the Baroque period. When the choir sang, "For unto us a child is born," the thought occurred to me that maybe this had more to do with what Christmas was about than the Santas, city lights, chestnuts and sleigh bells.

For some reason I didn't understand then and have never understood since, my childhood memories of Christmas past became as vivid as if they were taking place right there in the church. The image of my father clipping that light bulb onto our little Christmas tree suddenly brought a flood of tears into my eyes; so many that the handkerchief in my left front pocket could barely hold them all. Mona had no idea what was going on and I have never tried to explain it to her.

The pastor said some words about Jesus being born and, after she lit a candle on the big table at the front of the church, all the lights went dim and everyone sang, "Silent Night." I'm still not exactly sure what a "round yon virgin" is but the whole experience left me wondering if there was something about Christmas I had been missing out on all these years.

As we walked out of the church and back into the cold, humid air of late-December, downtown Manhattan, I pulled out my pocket calendar and pretended to flip it open.

I turned to Mona and said, "You know, the appointment I had set for tomorrow was cancelled this afternoon. How about I tag along with you to Jersey tomorrow?"

Mona didn't say anything. She just put her arm around me and didn't take it off until I kissed her good night at her apartment door.

Chapter 9

Snow

January

New York can be spectacular. In fact most of the time it *is* spectacular. But sometimes it can be beautiful, too. The clear spring air with fresh green foliage and the early flowers blooming in the Central Park Conservatory Garden is one of those times. But winter can be beautiful, too. At least on the days when the city is covered in fresh, dry snow and the bare limbs of trees are sheathed in white, silhouetted against a clear blue morning sky. The snow muffles the sound of traffic as the trucks, busses, cabs and cars slip and slide along the streets and avenues of Manhattan. That's when I wish they had sleigh rides in Central Park like they have carriage rides in the summer. Sometimes I see someone on cross-country skis leaving parallel tracks across what is usually a grassy meadow and, if it isn't a school day, neighborhood kids carry their sleds over to Pilgrim Hill.

Come to think of it, it is really only the city parks that are beautiful in the winter. There the snow stays white until it melts and disappears. In the asphalt jungle of man-made canyons, streets, gutters and concrete walkways, winter is most always nothing but slush spraying from passing vehicles into crowds of pedestrians or slush backing up into dirty glacial lakes behind the blocked grates of the city sewer system.

Today happened to be one of those beautiful winter mornings. Unfortunately, the only window I have in my apartment looks out over the air-well in the center of my building. There is nothing much to see except the occasional glimpse of someone else's life flitting past an un-curtained window.

I walked down two flights of stairs and joined the usual morning mass of humanity heading to work, to school or to god-only-knows-where. The collective clouds of warm, steamy exhalations rose into the air, adding extra layers of frost to the lower street-side windows and the cars whose owners had been lucky enough to find a place to park. My office was less than two blocks away. It was also on the second floor but unlike my apartment it had a one-window view of the street.

I could tell this would be one of those days I would find time to step away from my current investigations and take a walk in the park. I thought of calling Mona but she would be checking in for her day's work at the bookstore at 9:00. I had checked my voicemail before I left my apartment but once I was in the office I had to do it again with my answering machine.

There were two messages waiting for me at the office. The first was a friendly reminder from a client that he was still waiting for me to clear up his dispute with one of the larger department stores. I had tried to tell him that sometimes when you buy something and break it after you get home you can't expect the store to give you a refund when you return it. But he was willing to pay me to get his money back so once again I had sold my soul for a few bucks. The case had been on my back burner for two weeks and I couldn't argue the fact the guy had a point. I deserved a kick in the behind and I had gotten one . . . along with his threat to hire another PI so he could get his retainer back from me. I moved the case back up to the top of the list. It wasn't going to take me a lot of time to check it off anyway.

The other call was from my mother's sister, Lucille. When my mother left my father and me in the lurch back when I was six, Aunt Lucille tried to step in and save my father and me from our "sad and devastating time." She was the older of the two and had always considered my mother to be unsuited for anything, especially marriage and motherhood. She saw my mother's disappearance as her chance to prove to the world she was willing and able to take over and control our lives in the same way she had taken over and controlled her own husband and kids. My father would have nothing to do with Aunt Lucille. He told her she was a tyrannical busybody and he would have to be either insane or dead before he would let her stick her nose into our business which was none of hers. He kept true to his word until I was eighteen years old at which point he died and Aunt Lucille figured I was fair game.

Although I never had any reason to dislike her, I trusted my father's judgment in the matter and have done my best to keep as far away from her as possible. I have to admire her persistence, though. Every birthday and every holiday, I receive a card and sometimes a small gift. And, just like today, she occasionally calls me to let me know I am still in her thoughts and prayers. I have more of a guilt complex over my relationship with Aunt Lucille than anything else in my entire life. So of course I immediately hit the delete button on her message and hit rewind on my morning's business.

I phoned the department store manager's office and was transferred to customer service before I had a chance to demand a conversation with one of their lawyers. My explanation of my client's situation was met with a long silence followed by a slightly shorter sigh.

"I am so sorry," the very pleasant female voice said with a well-practiced hint of sadness, resignation and regret. "But we can't afford to offer a refund to every customer who buys a $1,200 cut-glass punchbowl and then drops it into a million pieces on the sidewalk in front of his house. We'd go broke."

The logic was flawless but I was being paid to be the guy's advocate so I used the only argument I had which was the threat of legal action.

Her response left me feeling as lame as Jacob felt after he lost his wrestling match with an angel.

"The small claims limit in New York is $5,000," she said. "I'm no expert and I probably shouldn't be giving my opinion on this but you wouldn't be eligible for a jury trial and no judge would give you more than five minutes before laughing you out of court. I don't think we would even need to have a lawyer represent us. We would probably just draft an official statement and send down one of our stockroom teenagers to read it to the judge. We would, of course, pay him minimum wage for his or her trouble. Your client would be left with paying you a large fee for the waste of your time and you would possibly be slapped with a contempt of court fine for wasting their time, too. But it's not my place to tell you what to do. Go ahead and do what you have to do. I couldn't care less. Good day."

And she hung up on me.

Sometimes if you dig way down deep into the soul of someone born and bred in Manhattan you will find some semblance of a heart. And sometimes you won't.

I called my client back and told him I was going to return his retainer in the afternoon mail. I also considered writing a letter commending the customer service representative to her supervisor. She was one heck of a firewall for malware like me. I never stood a chance.

Even though my finances were going backwards I took the time to bundle up, lock up the office and walk over to Central Park before the snow started to melt. Since it was a Saturday I decided to take the short walk to Pilgrim Hill and watch the kids having a good time. It's called Pilgrim Hill because there is a statue of one of the old-fashioned New England Pilgrims standing guard at the top. His face is shaded by an austere, broad-brimmed hat, which, on a day like today, makes him look like he is dressed more appropriately for a summer stroll than for sledding. On the other hand, his overcoat and cape looked heavy enough and, all considered, he was probably feeling warmer than I was. With his flintlock rifle firmly grasped in his right hand, he looked perfectly poised to chase the kids away if the snow pack fell short of the six inch minimum for sledding.

The kids didn't have to worry. There was plenty of snow on the ground and, despite the clear blue sky, the news predicted even more that night along with a sharp decrease in the already cold temperature. After five minutes of watching the children do the same thing over and over I headed back to 5th Avenue along the south side of the Metropolitan Museum of Art.

For Christmas Mona gave each of us annual passes to our two favorite museums which are, of course, the MoMA and the Metropolitan Museum of Art. It cost her almost a week's salary but I guessed her parents helped out with at least a part of it. I'm not convinced they approve of me as being everything their little girl deserves but they have welcomed me into their home and seem resigned to the fact I might possibly be a part of their family. *Satis est.*

Anyway, since I had the pass and was only a few steps from the front door of the Museum I decided to get out of the cold and see a friend or two before heading back to the office. Most of my family are in the MoMA, at least my mother is; front and center in Picasso's *Les Demoiselles d'Avignon.* But as for friends I have them hanging on walls and standing on pedestals all over Manhattan. Two of my best friends are in the Met.

Call me a snob but I am generally attracted to what is commonly referred to as "great art" or the "masterpieces." Over the years I have looked at famous paintings and I have looked at less famous paintings. I have decided that famous paintings are famous for a reason. They are famous because they are the best of the best. Over

152

hundreds of years, the cumulative judgment of critics usually gets it right. And the public, whether or not they can tell good art from bad, usually embraces the critic's verdict as their own.

The Met has more than its share of "great art." Nearly every gallery has at least one so-called "masterpiece." There are so many of them that most visitors flit through the museum following a recommended path so they can see as many of them in as short a time as possible. For me, that is heresy and blasphemy rolled into one. Paintings, more than any other medium, are like gracious hosts inviting us to enter their world and spend time with them. It is a serious breach of social etiquette to ogle them like a voyeur and then turn your back on them without at least saying 'Hello' and 'Thank you.'"

I am a big fan of the landscape painters. I guess you could say that Turner turns me on and Constable, especially his paintings of Salisbury Cathedral, in-"spires" me. But it is the portraits and the paintings with people close up and personal I like best. The way I see it, there are paintings you can look at and there are paintings you can talk to. Given the choice, I prefer the latter. So, of course, my two best friends in the Met are portraits'

The first is Rembrandt's *Self Portrait.* He painted over ninety of them and one of them hangs just down the street at the Frick. But it is the Met's I like best of all. Painted in 1660, the 54-year old painter stares full-face into our eyes. He looks serious and a little bit sad, as though he is carrying some heavy burden in his soul. Even so, he seems kindly enough, like someone's grandfather. If he was wearing clothing that was more contemporary, he could pass for one the older men who sometimes doze off in the pew-like seats in the museum lobby. I like to think he has adopted me as his grandson.

Like any good grandpa he prefers to ask me questions rather than give me answers. But I always have a pocketfull of questions to ask when I drop by for a visit. Today was no exception.

"Help me out here," I said from somewhere deep down inside. "You remember

Mona? My girl? Well, I think I want to marry her and I think she wants to marry me but she seems so noncommittal with the whole thing. She keeps telling me she loves me but that I need to get my life and priorities in synch before she can make up her mind about whether she wants to spend the rest of her life with me."

I paused to catch my breath. I listened but Grandpa Van Rijn seemed to be waiting for more.

"What advice do you have to give me? Be honest. I'm all ears."

I didn't have to wait long. Within a heartbeat I got the answer I knew I was going to get.

"Mike, listen to me. Mona seems like a nice girl and it would be a shame if you were to lose her."

There was a pause as if he was trying to choose his words carefully.

"In my opinion you should do exactly what she says. Get your life and priorities in synch. But just make sure you put her in the center of your life and make her your first priority. That is always the key to true love. You've got to move yourself into a supporting role and make your future wife the star of the whole production. And, if you don't mind me saying so, you should do the same thing with God."

I had always thought of Rembrandt as a humanist. His spiritual counsel caught me by surprise. I'd have to think about that later but, for the moment, what he said about me and Mona was spot on.

"Gee, thanks a lot," I said.

I really meant it. That's what real friends and grandfathers are for. To help you discover what you already know and to stand by you when you try to live it out.

Not too far away is Vermeer's painting, *Woman with a Pitcher*, also painted around 1660. I have been in love with her since before I hit my teens and, until I met Mona, she was the closest thing to a girl friend I ever had. The painting presents a moment frozen in time, as if some unseen person has stepped into the room and startled her. I like to think that the unseen person is me. She is clearly uncomfortable with me being there and responds by

155

averting her eyes and looking down and to her right. She is clearly a shy, introvert like me and that has always been part of her appeal. The warm light filtering in through the partially opened window contrasts with the cool blues of her dress and other objects in the room.

She is attractive but distant at the same time and bathed in melancholy. She seems to yearn for the touch of someone who would love her and who she could love in return. I had always hoped I was the person she was longing for. Since meeting Mona I think she looks just a little sadder than she did before. For some reason I have given her the name Frieda. I don't even know if it is a Dutch name but it seems to fit her somehow and she has never expressed any objection to it.

"Good afternoon, Frieda," I said. "I can't stay to talk today. I just wanted to say hello and see how you were doing."

She didn't say anything but she did raise her head just a bit and show the hint of a smile. Most of the time my friends just sit still the way they were painted. But sometimes, like this fleeing moment with Frieda, they become animated in ways that remind me of the paintings at Hogwarts in the Harry Potter movies. I smiled back and, with a kiss blown in her direction I turned and found my way out of the museum.

As I emerged outside onto the vast front-entrance stairway, I was hit by an arctic blast of cold air. In the short time I had been inside the temperature had dropped 10 degrees and the sky, which had been clear and blue, was rapidly becoming menacingly gray. By the time I got back to my office snowflakes were drifting down one at a time, as if they were in such short supply they had to be rationed. Since there were no more phone messages and nothing on my calendar for the rest of the day I called it quits and went back to my apartment.

I wanted to follow up on the advice I had gotten from Grandpa Van Rijn so I called Mona and told her that since tomorrow was Sunday, how about we go to church together and then head over to Rockefeller Plaza and eat lunch while we watched the skaters show off their spins and sitzmarks. She thought it was a good idea and thanked me for wanting to spend time with her. She can flash sarcasm with the best of them but her comment reminded me I still had a lot of work to do before I could "have" and "hold" her in married bliss.

What skipped my mind at that moment was that promises made are not always promises kept and that, in my chosen profession, priorities are subject to change at a moment's notice. And so it came to pass that on Sunday morning Mona found herself stiffed, and I didn't even remember to give her a call and tell her I wouldn't be showing up.

What happened is that my phone rang at 4:45 a.m. It was my friend Sid, who lets me borrow his car when I need one. Sid lives nearby but has a very different life-style than I do. First of all, he is raising his two children as a single Dad and, second, he rents a gorgeous ground floor, brownstone apartment with three bedrooms and a small backyard with a footpath, a garden and some lawn for the kids to play on. What Sid said on the phone was a bit convoluted but I managed to wake myself up enough to catch the gist of it.

It seems the night before he had thrown a party for a non-profit organization he volunteers for. They had completed their annual fund drive and had done very well. One person had donated an etching by Picasso; a signed original from his sexy and sensual Minotaur series. The etching was going to be auctioned off on Wednesday and had been placed on a table in the center of his living room so everyone could admire it and think about how much they might be willing to pay for it. Similar etchings have been auctioned or sold for $30,000 or more.

The party broke up at around 11:00 p.m. When the last person left at 11:15 the snow was just beginning to come down in earnest. Sid said he locked the doors and spent about forty-five minutes cleaning up before climbing into bed around midnight. At 4:30 a.m. he had gotten up to use the bathroom and thought he would take another peek at the Picasso. When he entered the living room the small table was still there but the etching was gone. He spent ten minutes looking around for it before deciding he would call me before calling the police.

"Please, can you come over right away?" he begged. "I'm in a big jam and need you to help me get out of it."

Completely forgetting my date with Mona I said, "Sure thing, pal. I'll be right over," and in ten minutes I was.

He let me in through the front door which, he said, had still been locked when he woke up. There were at least ten inches of pure, unadulterated snow on the front steps. It was clear no one had gone up or down them since it had started snowing the previous evening. I asked him about his two kids and he said, because of the party, they were spending the weekend with their mother. Inside he showed me where the etching had been. We

158

looked around in the kitchen, bathrooms, bedrooms, dining area and even the coat closet by the front door. Nothing.

I asked if anyone had a key to the door and he said, "So far as I know, the only ones with keys besides me are my brother in Hoboken and the owner of the building."

Whoever got into the apartment either had a key or could walk through walls. The key theory seemed more likely so I asked him for the names and phone numbers of the suspects.

After thinking things through for a few moments I changed my mind and said, "Sid, this is a big deal and I'm not sure I'm the guy to be doing this. I think you need to bring in the NYPD."

He looked down and around, and rolled his eyes and said, "I guess you're right. The company that insures the etching might not pay up if they could find some way to discredit you . . . nothing personal, of course."

"Don't worry about it," I said. "Just call the cops. Maybe they'll find fingerprints or something."

Sid responded by saying "Okay" and by dialing 911.

The dispatcher said she would let the local precinct know and someone would be over sooner or later that morning

Sid fixed some coffee and we talked about the non-profit and how upset everyone was going to be, including the donor and the insurance company. It was a little past 6:00 a.m. and I told Sid there was nothing more I could do so I would take my leave and go home.

Before walking to the front door I said, "If you need a witness to give testimony regarding the etching's *post mortem* feel free to give me a call any time of any day."

As I stepped out of the front door the first hint of a winter sunrise added a subtle glow to the piled snow. Out on the road the snow had already been reduced to a dirty slush but the apartment steps and parts of the adjacent sidewalk were still untouched by any feet but my own. Someone who must have been a neighbor was working his way across the front of Sid's apartment with a snow shovel. He waved a friendly "good morning" and, as I was waving back, I froze in a pose that looked more like the Statue of Liberty than it did Mike Maurison, Private Eye.

"Stop shoveling," I yelled. "Step back and don't move."

I knocked on Sid's door and when he answered, I asked him for a whiskbroom if he had one. He found one and asked what was going on.

I said, "Step outside with me for a moment."

The guy with the snow shovel was still standing there like the Venus de Milo except with both arms intact. His shoveling had given me an idea I hoped would solve this case before the police showed up.

"Sid," I said. "Check this out,"

I pointed down the stairs to where the sidewalk had been shoveled.

"What do you see?" I asked.

"I don't know," he said. "Piles of shoveled snow, a partially cleared sidewalk and . . . I don't know . . . what am I supposed to see?"

I pointed to three white splotches on the sidewalk. "Can you tell me what those are?" I asked.

"Well," Sid guessed, "I suppose they are compacted snow from someone's shoes. What's the point?"

I explained the footprints were leading away from his apartment steps. I reminded him what he had said about the snow just starting to fall heavily when the guests left at 11:00 p.m. In response to a question, he assured me the snow had not yet covered the sidewalk or the steps when he said "Goodnight" to the last one. And here is when I got to show off a little.

I began sweeping Sid's front steps with the whisk. My footprints coming up the steps were obvious. But buried under the snow were more footprints like the ones on the sidewalk. The foot prints all went down the steps. There were none coming up but mine.

"What this means," I said, "is the owner of these footprints must have come up the steps before 'the snow lay on the ground, cool and crisp and even.'"

Sid looked confused so I went on.

"But the person went down the steps after the snow had started falling. Later, as the snow continued to fall, the footprints were covered up and disappeared until your neighbor brought them to light with his shovel."

Sid scratched his head and said, "I don't get it. What are you trying to tell me?"

"Elementary, my dear Sid," I replied. "These prints tell me who stole the etching and how they did it."

Sid shook his head "No" but he said, "Okay, explain yourself."

So I did.

"One of the people who attended your party didn't leave when the others did," I explained. "They hid themselves in the apartment somewhere, in the coat closet or your kid's bedroom and then waited until you went to bed and fell asleep. Then they walked into the living room, picked up the etching, put it in a bag of some sort, and walked out the front door, closing it behind them still locked as though it had been locked from the inside.

"It was a perfect crime except for one thing: While they were waiting for you to fall asleep it started snowing outside. When they left they left their footprints in the snow, perfectly revealing their shoe size and type of shoe. From the look of these prints, I would say they were left by a pair of size 7 women's high heels. Does that remind you of anyone who was at your party last night?"

It did and, when the cops showed up ten minutes later I had them take pictures of the footprints and explained what I thought about the whole thing. As a kindness to Sid, I stayed around until the police finished their work and had taken down all the information the two of us could given them.

When they had left I said, "Well, Sid. My guess is you are going to have your etching back very soon and that you will also be losing one of your nonprofit's wanna-be patrons."

I may have sounded like the slip of paper in a fortune cookie but, if I had been playing the lottery I would have been a millionaire. As it turned out I had, in fact, solved the case before the police had shown up.

Once again Sid owed me big time. A few minutes more and all those beautiful footprints would have been shoveled up or trampled under the feet of all those cops going up and down the steps. As they say, "Timing is everything." And today my timing had been perfect.

I started to ask Sid if he wanted to go somewhere for breakfast but before the first word fell out of my mouth I remembered Mona. I tried calling her cell phone but there was no answer except for her voice mail. It dawned on me she had turned it off before the church service started.

I ran all the way to 5th Avenue and caught the bus south. It dropped me off right in front of the church. I wasn't dressed well enough to be mistaken for an usher but I did manage to find Mona sitting in her usual pew with her head bowed while the pastor was giving what turned out to be a surprisingly short prayer. As I sidled up next to her the organ broke in and everyone stood up and began singing "Amazing Grace." I know Mona saw me but she didn't acknowledge I was there. It crossed my mind this was probably how my Aunt Lucille felt every time I ignored her. I considered giving my aunt a return call sometime in the coming week but, at the moment, my first priority was to get things right with Mona . . . again.

The pastor preached a short sermon on one of Jesus' parables; the one about the master who forgave the large debt one of his servants owed him and then how that same servant turned around and threatened another servant with jail if he didn't pay back the piddling amount he had lent him. The Master heard about it and called the first servant into his office, called him "wicked" and had him thrown in jail because he was willing to be forgiven but was not willing to forgive someone else.

Maybe it was because of the sermon and maybe it wasn't. But in any case, after the service Mona acted as though I had met her as planned and had been with her when she walked into church a half-hour before I actually showed up. I felt terrible, of course, but I knew I had hooked onto a real gem in Mona. Once again she had proven to be the sort of person I could only dream of being myself.

As we walked to Rockefeller Plaza she took my hand in hers. Somehow we managed to get seats for lunch right next to the window overlooking the ice skating rink. I suppose the skaters were out there whirling and twirling but I never really noticed any of it. I was spending the whole time looking at Mona and loving her more than ever.

Chapter 10

A Window In the Door
February

Some days I think maybe I should get a window installed in my office door. It would have to be the kind that's one-way since the door leads right into the hall. That way I could see who was trying to come in before they actually got in. Not that I would ever lock anyone out, of course. I'll take money from anybody if they have it. And it's not really about safety, either. I have never been raped, robbed or assaulted by anyone yet; at least not in my office. Now that I'm thinking about it I suppose I'd have to pay someone to put "Mike Maurison —Private Eye" on the glass with some of those high-class shiny gold letters. I'm not cheap or anything but I usually don't have much dough to throw around except for food and rent.

Part of the problem is that I'm not the only person in the building. There is a beauty salon on the ground floor and a few other offices next to mine on the second. But most of the rooms on my floor and everything above are flats and apartments with lots of people walking around day and night. A glass window might tempt some loser to break in and look around for something valuable. Even if I owned anything valuable, I wouldn't leave it sitting around in my office. The only exception is the Blue Bersa .380 I usually leave locked in one of my desk drawers when I'm not wearing it on a case somewhere.

Today turned out be one of those days when I wish I had put the window in my door. The voice on the street door intercom sounded slightly slurred but I buzzed the guy in. Like everybody else that hits my buzzer I assumed he needed me to either "find something" or "find out about something." That, of course, is what I get paid to do. But this particular guy hadn't read the script. When I let him into my office he turned out to be tall, thin and ragged around the edges. His hair was straggly and greasy, streaked with gray and tied back in a pony tail with a rubber band. His glasses were lopsided and held together by some bandage tape wound around the nose bridge. The soles on his tennis shoes were flapping like the tails of the dolphins they used to have at the New York Aquarium at Coney Island. He also smelled as though he had been sleeping in a pile of Limburger cheese for the past two weeks. If my office had ever had a new car smell it was going to be gone forever in a few minutes. I knew right off I would be smelling this guy for the next month unless I got him out as fast as possible. But since I am a schmuck I pretended to be nice and did everything I could not to gag or to hold my hand over my nose.

"So," I began with muted sarcasm, "what brings you here this fine, sunny afternoon?"

To my surprise, when he spoke he didn't sound at all like he looked.

"I would be very grateful, sir, if you could find something for me."

"Sure, I'll give it a try if you can make it worth my while. What are you looking for?"

"My dignity and a home."

Yes, that is what he said. The words went into my ears and jangled around making the inside of my head echo like the sound you get in the Holland Tunnel if you are stupid enough to open your car window. Eventually the words broke apart and formed new ones as they came out of my mouth. As usual, what came out was not exactly what I had planned on.

"And where, my good man, did you last see them?" is what I said.

I was immediately embarrassed and ashamed for saying this but the man didn't seem to mind at all.

"I lost them some years ago, back in California when I was discharged from the U.S. Army. The military had been my home and my dignity for over twenty years. I have been homeless and destitute ever since. I don't want to live like this anymore. The sign outside says you are a 'private eye.' I assume that means you can find things. Will you take me as a client? I would be most grateful."

"If you don't mind my asking a question first," I replied. "I'm thinking that after twenty years in the military . . . don't you receive a pension or something?"

What I meant of course was, "If I help you will you be able to pay me anything?" But once again his answer surprised me.

"As a matter of fact, I do. I retired with the rank of Captain. Not the Navy kind; that would be a higher rank. But a retired Army Captain does get something. Not enough to live on, but enough to supplement other earnings, investments and Social Security when he is old enough to collect it."

They guy was starting to sound like one of those retirement financial planners who tries to get you to buy an "inflation-proof and guaranteed-ten-percent-annual-interest-for-life" annuity. What this guy was trying to sell I hadn't figured out. But he kept on talking as if he hadn't had the chance to talk with someone for a long time.

"At the present time I have made arrangements for the direct deposit of my military retirement into a low-risk mutual fund I hold with Franklin-Templeton. It's there if I need it. But that's not why I came here today. My money might buy me a 'house,' but not a 'home.' And there will never be enough of it to cover the cost of my dignity. For my dignity is more valuable than life itself. My very soul would wither before I could buy or sell my dignity . . . ."

"Stop it, stop it!" I interrupted. "What you're asking from me is impossible. You might as well be the Tin Man from the *Wizard of Oz* asking for a heart. You know you can't get it from anyone but yourself. I think the same is true for dignity. Somewhere out there is your personal Yellow Brick Road. If you follow it I'm sure that someday you'll find your dignity and get back to your Kansas home. You and your little dog, too."

I was finished and done with this pathetic lunatic and I was tired of his idiotic prattling . . . not to mention being overwhelmed by the smell. I hoped he would take the hint and excuse himself but, of course, he didn't.

"As you know," he countered, "the Tin Man did not discover his heart alone by himself. He had the Wizard, who sent him on a quest, and he had faithful friends who accompanied him and helped him discover the heart of love he had possessed from the beginning."

His own words stopped him in a way that mine could not. He paused for a moment and I had the funny feeling that if he had been sprayed with silver paint he would have looked almost exactly like Jack Haley. The pause ended, he straightened himself up to his full height and gave a small bow in my direction.

"My dear friend, your words have done more for me than you will ever know. You have helped me to understand that I never actually lost my dignity at all. It has been with me all along."

Here he put his hand across his chest as if he was saying the "Pledge of Allegiance."

"And," he continued, "a house can become a home if it is allowed to become a place where people live and love each other."

This time, instead of giving a bow he directed a sharp military salute in my direction. I was tempted to return the salute but, not having served in the military, I wasn't sure it would be appropriate.

In any case, he stepped forward, reached into his back pocket and pulled out what looked like a beat up version of the small photo albums women carry in their purses so they can show off pictures of their grandchildren. I have no idea whether there were any photos in it but he pulled out a $100 bill and wordlessly

169

handed it to me. Then he did an "about face" in the proper military way, opened my office door and marched out and down the hall. I never saw or heard from him again. To this day I don't know whether he was completely nuts or, in some strange way, more sane than I am. What I do know is it was a pleasant surprise to find that his malingering, malodorous smell disappeared from my office in less than two days.

With a hundred bucks in hand I decided to call it a day. I called Mona and asked if she could take the rest of the afternoon off. She asked her supervisor at the bookstore who told her no, not today.

Fridays are usually busy at Benson's Books and Things but I had time on my hands so I walked the seven blocks just so say "Hi." When I went in it wasn't really crowded at all so I went over to the Children's Section, picked up a worn out "Please Read Me a Story" copy of *The Tales of Hans Christian Andersen* and sat down on one of the carpeted benches they use for Children's Story Hour on Saturday mornings.

Mona has worked her way up to being the Assistant Manager for Customer Service. It is a pretentious title and it means she gets to talk with the folks who come in and help them find what they are looking for. She also handles returns, complaints and disinfects the headphones in the CD section after they've been used. She works thirty-five hours a week which is just barely enough to pay for food and rent for the two-bedroom apartment she shares with two other girls.

The book in my hand fell open to the story of "Thumbelina" which tells about a micro-miniature girl trying to survive in a monstrously large world of toads,

170

moles, dung beetles and mice. After many adventures and terrifying escapes she fortuitously meets a handsome fairy prince who marries her and presents her with a pair of wings like his own.

I looked out the bookstore window at the towering buildings that dwarfed the people scurrying up and down the street. From the top of the taller buildings people would look like Thumbelinas and fairy princes searching for one another. Imagining Mona as Thumbelina was easy but imagining myself as a fairy prince . . . well, that was not so easy.

I jumped a bit as someone's arm draped itself around my neck from behind and someone's lips gave me a warm, moist kiss on my ear.

I prayed to God it was Mona and, of course, my prayer was answered with, "What are doing here? Let me guess . . . You're having trouble solving a case and you came here to get some advice from Encyclopedia Brown. Am I right?"

I stood up smiling and returned her greeting with a small puff of warm breath on her ear. She giggled and said since it was time for her afternoon break she could take a minute to tell me something that had happened earlier that morning.

It seems two plainclothes cops from the Narcotics Division had rushed in and grabbed some guy who had just walked into the store. The guy didn't put up a fight and acted as if the whole thing was a joke. They stood him against a wall and gave him a thorough pat-down. After fifteen minutes a police van with flashing lights pulled up and a uniformed officer came in with a German Shepherd that sniffed all over the store but only seemed interested in giving off small yips whenever they brought him near the kid who by now had been cuffed and was sitting on the floor. The cops did a lot of talking to each other and the one who seemed to be in charge spent a lot of time talking on a cell phone to somebody who must have been calling all the shots. After about forty-five minutes they took the guy away in a squad car, the dog and his handler got back in the van and, after apologizing to the manager and exchanging contact information, the narcs left.

The manager told the staff the cops had been tailing this guy for days. They had seen what they thought had been a drug transaction on the Central Park side of Fifth Avenue and East 72nd and followed the guy across the street. But just before he came to the bookstore he looked behind him and must have sensed something wasn't kosher. He ducked in the door and they grabbed him next to the Fantasy and Science Fiction section. They said they could have sworn they had seen him put something in his pocket but except for something only the dog could smell, he was as clean as a G-Rated movie. If any of us thought of something that might be of help they wanted us to give them a call. They also said they might be back.

I put the book down and asked Mona if the store had any security cameras running that morning.

"Yes we do," she said.

"Is there some way I could see what's on them? I mean, like, right now? If the cops know their stuff they should be back to grab them with a warrant before you close shop this evening. I'd like to beat them to it if you don't mind."

Mona had a few words with the manager who then came over to have a few words.

172

"Mike," she said. "What the hell do you think you're doing nosing into what's none of your business?"

"This *is* my business," I told her with a smile. "This is what I do for a living."

At this point, I struck a Napoleonic pose and continued with my best stentorian affectation.

"And I will do it *gratis* as a favor to this wonderful city that produces enough crooks and slime balls to keep me in business."

I returned to my everyday voice and added with a wink, "What do you say? Can I have a sneak peek?"

She muttered something under her breath and wiggled her finger at me as a sign to follower her. We ended up in the back of the store in a little cubicle next to the stockroom. There was a chair, a small desk and an even smaller video screen that flipped running images from several store surveillance cameras as if they were a slide show. She poked a few buttons and brought the screen to where the time 10:15 a.m. showed in the upper right corner.

"Here, this is just before he came into the store. Let's see how good a gumshoe you are."

She showed me how to run the video from each camera separately and, after a few minutes, I had seen everything I needed to see.

"Who's this guy walking out of the store at 10:17 when the other guy was being tackled to the floor by the cops?"

Mona answered first, "Oh, that's Phil. He's in charge of the stock room. He comes in at night, gets all the inventory up-to-date, opens and sorts through all the previous day's deliveries and puts all the stock in order

173

for the next day's business. He usually leaves between 10 or 10:30. Why do you ask?"

"If my hunch is right then I think he's the one the cops will want to be talking to."

I stood up and Mona and the manager followed me across the store to the Fantasy and Science Fiction section. The suspect had walked down this aisle just before the cops rushed him, and right where I thought it would be there was a place where a few books had been pushed back three or four inches. In front of them, stuck on the shelf, was a small red dot, the sort of sticker that goes on the spine of a book when it goes on the Bargain Table.

"It may not be an 'X' but it does mark the spot," I said. "The only person who walked down this aisle between the time the suspect walked down it and the cops showed up was Phil. The guy didn't come in here to hide from the cops. He came in here to make a drop—and it was well planned, too. Someone must have told him something like "Benson's . . . red dot in the F&SF aisle."

"Out of habit, he turned to look behind him just before he turned into the store. He didn't see the cops at all but they thought he did. All he had to do was walk down the correct aisle where the security cameras could only see his head and shoulders, find the red dot, make sure there was no one standing there watching, and put whatever he had in his pocket down on the dot.

"Within fifteen seconds Phil comes by, picks it up, puts it in his pocket and, without missing a beat or attracting any notice, walks right past the cops, right out the door and disappears right down the street. Pretty slick if you ask me. No wonder the suspect was laughing. The first ten seconds he was in the store was the only time he was out of the sight of those cops. There was no other place or time he could have made the drop."

The manager added a thought, "That makes sense, doesn't it. Phil has spent a lot of time in that security room and probably knows everything that can be seen or not seen by those cameras. He would know the best possible place to do something like this; and in broad daylight in a store full of customers, too!"

"But," she went on, "It's hard for me to believe Phil would be involved in something like this. He's always been such a good worker."

"Well," I said, "I don't have anything more to say except to make it clear I haven't proven anything. I've just put the facts together in a way that might explain what happened here this morning. It'll be up to the NYPC to see if they can make a case out of it. Give me a few minutes and I'll write it down for you to give to the cops."

I did, they did, the police followed up with an investigation and both Phil and the suspect were busted, charged, found guilty, scolded by the court, released on probation, and I got to be the fairy prince who saved the day and got the girl.

The next day Mona and I dropped by the Museum of Modern Art for a short visit to see some of the oil- and water-based members of my family and friends. Our friend Robert greeted us at the front door which was a surprise since he usually has Saturdays off. On this particular morning he seemed more animated than usual. He even seemed glad to see us.

"Good morning, Robert," I said. "How's tricks?"

175

I can't say I had ever seen Robert smile before but the hint of one flickered just long enough for me to notice as he held up his left hand and wiggled his ring finger.

There was nothing on it so I had to ask, "What's up with the finger thing?"

I could see he was fighting back an even bigger smile, one that was trying to erupt out of his face like Mt. St. Helens. He finally gave up and let it come out.

"It's Chia," he said. "I gave her a ring."

There was a pause while the smile dimmed just a bit.

It returned in full force when he added, "I don't mean 'ring' like a phone call. I mean a real ring, the kind you wear on your finger. Pretty neat, huh? She actually said, 'Yes' to me!"

I slapped him on the back and Mona gave him a soft poke on the arm. We were all smiling and the words "How wonderful" and "Congratulations" got all mixed in with "When did it happen?" and "Have you set a date yet?" and "Last night" and "No, not yet."

An elderly couple came through the door and Robert's smile disappeared as fast as a snowflake on hot asphalt. It didn't return but he did give us a wink before becoming his usual, stoic self again.

"Let's all get together again sometime soon, okay?" I asked.

With his normal air of indifference, he shrugged his shoulders and said, "Sure."

Mona said she would give Chia a call and set it up and Robert shoved his hands in his pockets and unintentionally did his best "Aw Shucks" imitation of Will Rogers.

176

Mona and I went up to the Fifth Floor to see if the gallery had changed any of the exhibits but everything looked the same as usual. Mom still pretended to stare dispassionately at me from her place at the center of Picasso's *Les Demoiselles d'Avignon* even though I knew how glad she was to see me.

I said,"Hi" to her in my usual way and let her know everything was all right with me and with Mona, too.

Mona, who knows all there is to know about me and Mom gave her regards. We stood and looked at some of the paintings for a while, took the elevator back down, said *sayonara* to Robert and caught the bus back to our part of town in the Upper East Side.

As we got off at Fifth Avenue and 68th Mona took my hand and led me across the street to Central Park. She found an empty bench and, with our breath making plumes of steam in the chill, late winter air, we sat down.

The bench was cold and the chill came right through our clothes.

Mona cuddled up close against me for a moment before asking, "You know, I think it's wonderful that Robert and Chia are getting married, don't you?"

Inside I squirmed a little. After all, I am a private eye and there were plenty of clues to show me where this conversation was heading.

"Of course I do. I am very happy for Robert; and for Chia, too."

"Robert seems so much happier than when I first met him last September. That was right after he met Chia, wasn't it? And right before I me you."

I tried to choose my words carefully, with the same fear and trepidation a man feels when he's trying to choose a gift to give his wife for her birthday.

"Are you trying to figure out if I've changed at all since I met you?"

"Not really," Mona replied. "I know you've changed. And I'm glad for every one of those changes, especially the ones that have drawn us closer together. I'm not really sure I'm asking anything at all. I've just been thinking about us—you and me—and whether there is a future for us or whether we're just meant to be together for the 'here and now.'"

I could tell she had hit a serve and the ball was now on my side of the court, so I took a swing and hit a lob perfectly placed for an overhand slam down my throat.

"I am very happy with the 'here and now,' aren't you?"

After a moment, she stopped cuddling and looked me straight in the eye.

"What do you mean by that?" She demanded.

"I don't know what I mean," I stammered, knowing she had me point, set and match. "Do you want to move into my apartment with me? It's a mess but we could clean it up and . . . ."

At that she stood up and said, "No. I do not want to move in with you. Not now and maybe never unless you figure out how I am supposed to fit into your life. At the moment I'm cold and tired and . . . and . . . I'll talk to you later . . . maybe."

She timed her departure in perfect synch with the green pedestrian crossing light. She was gone and I suddenly remembered just how cold the park bench was.

As a matter of fact I felt cold all the way home and felt cold even after I had turned up the heat in my apartment.

Dames, I said to myself. The only thing I could think of was to add, *You can't live with 'em and you can't live without 'em.* But I knew that cliché was a lie the moment I thought it. I had spent twelve years alone without a mother, a father or any family that mattered to me. I hadn't even had a girlfriend who really mattered until Mona came along, Somehow I had slipped into imagining things could just keep on the way they were. Sort of along the lines of, "If it ain't broke, don't fix it."

It was clear to me now that something was broken and that it would be up to me to decide whether I wanted to fix it or not. I could have blamed Robert and Chia for screwing everything up but I knew it didn't have anything to do with them. It was all about Mona and me.

I looked around my apartment and noticed for the first time just how much of a dump it was. I remembered a quote from St. Bernard-not-the-dog who said, "What we love we shall grow to resemble." I knew that I did not want to keep looking like my apartment. If I wanted to start looking more like Mona then I would have to start loving her at least as much as I loved myself or maybe even more than that. I felt I had reached a crossroads and had to choose which way I would go. It was one of the loneliest and most emotional moments of my life. I sat down on my sofa and cried until I couldn't cry any more.

When I woke up it was past midnight. Somehow while I was sleeping my decision had been made and I couldn't wait another minute to talk to Mona.

When she answered her phone she said, "Its one o'clock in the morning! What is wrong with you!"

I assumed the question was rhetorical but as it turned out, she really meant it.

After a few more choice comments from her end I finally managed to say, "Mona, listen to me. There is nothing wrong with me except that I am in love with you and want to spend the rest of my life with you. The thought of you leaving me is not something I want to imagine ever again. Will you marry me?"

I heard something that might have been a cell phone disconnecting, but I waited and waited, hoping she was still there trying to figure out how to answer my question.

"Mike," she finally said, and I held my breath to hear what she was going to say, "Mike, I would like to marry you. But I am not going to say 'Yes' until we have talked this thing through from beginning to end. Now, good night, and go to sleep."

At that moment, I was more awake than I had ever been in my life, but it only took me a few minutes to fall into one of the deepest, healing, and refreshing sleeps I had ever enjoyed.

In the morning, Manhattan was smothered in an icy, dense, smoggy cloud that hid the sun and transformed the city into a gray-scale image in a two-dimensional world.

But my heart soared as if it knew that this first day of the week was going to be the first day of the rest of my life. There had been a fork in the road and, like Yogi Berra, I took it.

180

Chapter 11

More than Meets the Eye

March

As a private eye, my job is to find things and solve puzzles for people. Cameras make my job easier and because of that I have taken up an interest in them.

It was a Wednesday afternoon. I was waiting for Mona to finish her day's work at the bookstore and was leafing through a photo book of Abraham Lincoln. Two photos caught my attention. Lincoln wasn't in them but he could have been if they had been taken the night before. The pictures were taken in Ford's Theater the day after Lincoln was shot. One showed the box he had been sitting in, still decked out with patriotic bunting. The other showed the now-empty stage with the central door, still ajar, that Booth had limped through after jumping from Lincoln's box to the stage.

I read somewhere that after the invention of the camera the first people to take photos of crime scenes and criminals were the French. During the 1880s a

Frenchman named Alphonse Bertillon actually attempted to turn the process into a scientific art form. The mug shot with full-face and profile was his invention.

But here at Ford's Theater were two crime scene photos from way back in 1865. They do not reveal anything of forensic significance but they do serve as a sort of time-machine allowing us to revisit the scene of the crime. They are strangely empty of people except for the ghostly blur of a Union Soldier standing in the box adjacent to Lincoln's. Early cameras required such a long exposure that a person walking past would be either a fuzzy smudge or completely invisible when the picture was developed.

Now that I have a smart phone, I can use it to take snapshots or videos on a moment's notice. For stakeouts, I have a digital camera that includes video for action scenes and an infrared setting for night photos. It has worked well enough to send several crooks to jail; caught in the act when they thought the darkness was their friend.

Mona came over when she was done and we walked over to Central Park to stretch our legs and get away from the noise of traffic for a few minutes.

"Well Mr. Mike Maurison, Private Eye, anything new today?" Mona asked.

"Nothing much," I said, "I suppose it isn't a breach of confidence to tell you I've been contracted by an insurance outfit. I'm supposed to check out whether some guy is really injured or not. Nothing new about it, though. In my business it's a routine investigation. He's claiming a back injury, wears a rigid back brace and is filing a claim with his former employer as well as applying for

SSI. The bottom line is I've got to do some surveillance later this evening."

"Oh," Mona sounded disappointed. "I guess that ends my plan to go to a movie tonight. We haven't done anything together for weeks except eat out and talk on the phone."

"Well," I said with a smile, "I've been thinking about that, too. That's why I bought two cheap seat matinee tickets to Lincoln Center for this Sunday. It's *Carmen*, one of my favorite operas."

"Mine, too. I think . . . " Mona said, looking doubtful. "That's the one about the lady and the bullfighter by Ravel, right?"

"Well, sort of," I replied. "The lady and the bullfighter parts are right but the composer was Bizet."

At this point, I begin belting out a very bad rendition of "Toreador" with lots of "la-la-las" where I couldn't remember the words.

Mona smiled and said, "I'm glad you aren't in the cast. I'd probably ask for my money back!"

She stopped walking and gave me a big hug and a sloppy kiss right in front of the Alice in Wonderland statue.

"Thank you for the tickets. I do love you, you know"

"I know it," I said. "But it's nice to hear it out loud once in a while. I love you too, even though you haven't bought me any tickets lately."

Mona laughed again.

"That's because you have more money than I do! Right now I'd have to pawn my full set of Sister Wendy art books to pay for an opera ticket."

That's one of the things I like about Mona. She likes art almost as much as I do. When we first met I used to kid her about her name because it reminded me of the words "moan and groan," but she came right back at me and said, "The next time you hear my name think about this: If you change just one letter it would spell MoMA."

I have to say that made my attitude make a u-turn. I used to love her in spite of her name. Now I love her because of it!

Mona graduated from NJCU in Jersey City with a major in English Lit and has taken most of the classes required for a Masters in Library Science at CUNY Queens. The bookstore job suits her well but she really would like to land a civil service position in the NY Public Library system. She also has applied for a job at the Hunter College Library just down the street from the bookstore.

My degree is in Mechanical Engineering but I was afraid if I ever designed and built something it would fall down. So, for some reason I have never figured out I decided to enter the Private Eye business. Three years of night school studying law enforcement, criminal law and how to solve stuff helped get me qualified to pass my PI license exam. I have a permit to carry a gun, too, but I almost always leave it in the desk drawer in my office. I am a big Monty Python fan and am willing to "Run away! Run away!" at the drop of a hat.

Both Mona and I would rather be in a museum than anywhere else in the world. We are both jealous of our friend Robert who gets to work at the Museum of Modern Art. The job gives him free access to virtually every other museum in the City. As they say, his pay isn't much but the benefits are wonderful. In any case, we also share interests in music, the theater and, of course, pizza. We walked back to the bookstore and parted ways like Paul and Barnabas did during their first missionary journey— except on friendlier terms.

My journey took me in the direction of my apartment where I needed to grab my camera and a jacket for what was likely going to be a long night out on the town. As I walked, all I could think about was Mona. Our earlier conversations about getting married had come to a screeching halt when Mona decided my attempt to propose to her over the phone at 1:00 in the morning— after having a blow-out argument over the future of our relationship—did not seem to offer an encouraging start to a commitment she wanted to last a lifetime.

"When the time is right, we'll both know," she said. "And if and when that time comes, I will say, 'Yes.'"

It had sounded like a good plan, but afterwards, the only thing I could remember was her use of the word, "if."

After getting what I needed from my apartment, I took the subway up to 116th and transferred to a bus that took me over to Lenox in Harlem. The guy I was supposed to check out lived five blocks away. The insurance people said he worked at a nearby corner market so I decided to see what he was able to do when he thought no one was looking.

He came out of his apartment door at 6:15 p.m. and began walking. Every so often he would pause, put his hand on his back, look around and take a deep breath. Ten minutes later, he walked into the store where he talked to the cashier for a few minutes before taking charge of the place by himself. He spent most of the next five and a-half hours sitting in a tall chair behind the cash register. Every so often, he would come around the counter to help a customer and once he locked the front door for a couple of minutes while I assume he went to the bathroom. His shift ended at midnight so I left five minutes early to set up something in front of his apartment. I figured he would walk straight back after he left the market but he never showed up. I was feeling frustrated when I made the trip back to my place in the Upper East Side afterward.

The next evening I did the same thing except this time I borrowed my friend Sid's car. At 11:15 p.m. I drove back to Harlem, parked up the street from the market and waited until the guy left the store at five past midnight. As I suspected, he didn't walk home this time either. A beat-up Nissan Sentra pulled up and he got in. I followed the car over to East Harlem where my man got out, bent all the way to the ground, stood back up again and slid open a large, heavy gate. The car pulled into a parking area between two car dealerships. After the gate was closed, the two men opened a door and disappeared into one of the buildings.

I learned two things that night. First, I learned that if the guy really had a back injury he could turn it on and off whenever he wanted to. And he could take the brace on and off whenever he wanted as well. Second, I noticed the two men didn't need to unlock the door before they went in which meant one or more people were already inside. I didn't have a chance to take a photo that night but I knew I would be able to get one tomorrow or the next day if I was patient and clever enough.

186

I spent Thursday writing up a few case summaries and doing research on a 19th century sailing vessel a client believed held the secret to his family's arrival in America from Buenos Aries. Genealogy is a booming business and if I can make some money looking for missing limbs on family trees I will gladly grab a vine and swing through the branches like Tarzan looking for a banana.

Friday I spent the whole day checking out my man in Harlem. I spent the morning casually meandering around the guy's neighborhood trying my best not to look like I was up to no good. Just before noon, my patience was rewarded when the guy's door opened and he walked over to where Lenox turns into Malcolm X Blvd. Like before, he stopped every so often, put his hand on his back and looked around. He bought a newspaper and what looked like some lottery tickets at a liquor store and then went into a barber shop where I assumed he was going to get a haircut. When I walked past and looked in the window all the chairs were empty and he was nowhere in sight. The sign on the door said "Closed for Lunch—Back at 1:00 p.m." At one o'clock, he came out with his hair as scruffy as before and headed back towards his apartment. I put a piece of gum in my mouth and started chewing. I had a head start and beat him home by half a block. At the bottom of the stairs going up to his apartment building door I put the gum onto a $20 bill and stuck it to the cement.

With my camera in hand, I watched him walk up to the stairs, look down and then look around. Stiffly and with some effort he bent over and laid his newspaper on the ground. He took off his jacket and removed the back brace he was wearing underneath. He then bent over as nicely as you please and picked up the twenty bucks. When he was part-way up the stairs the back brace slipped out of his hand and bounced down a couple of steps. He didn't even bother to walk down to it. He just bent over like a folding chair and picked it up two steps below where he was standing. I got it all on video. He had fallen for one of the oldest tricks in the P.I. book.

The investigation was off to a good start but I still needed more to show this hadn't been a one-time fluke.

That night I was ready for him. I had cased the car dealer that afternoon and knew right where to stand to get a good photo if the opportunity presented itself. Just like before, at five minutes past midnight the Nissan pulled up to the store and drove off with Mr. Back-Brace. I took a few back streets I had researched on Google maps and got there a couple of minutes before they did. To my disappointment, the brightly-lit gate was wide open. Once they went inside the dealership I could see them moving around through the big plate-glass windows . . . but only barely because they had left all the lights turned off. I was too far away for infrared but I snapped a few infrared photos and took a video through my telephoto lens anyway, just in case. I then tried some long time exposures in regular light but was not too optimistic about them either. At 1:15 a.m., they got back into the car and headed back towards Lenox. I didn't bother to follow them. I went home, put the car back where it belonged and went to sleep.

When I woke up on Saturday, I skipped breakfast and downloaded my surveillance photos onto my computer. The infrared video and photos showed bodies standing or moving around like the aliens in *Close Encounters*. The time-exposure photos looked like the daguerreotype photos of Ford's Theater I had seen in the book. Because the people in the building had been moving around the whole time there were some nice photos of the interior of the showroom but no images of people at all. One showed someone as a slight blur, looking something like the Union Solder standing in the theater box next to Lincoln's. For all practical purposes my stage was as empty as the one John Wilkes Booth had broken his leg on. As far as my photographs were concerned science and technology had failed to move me out of the mid-nineteenth century.

The nice thing about digital photography is you can take as many pictures as you want without wasting film. If you don't like a photo you can delete it without any muss or fuss. Because of this, I had taken fifteen shots at more or less the same setting I would have used without a flash in a less than brightly lit room. When I downloaded them they showed up more or less completely black except for some reflection on the showroom glass from surrounding street and security lights.

Photoshop gave me an idea so I tried lightening them up. They got grainier but, after a while the figures in the room became visible. The telephoto lens had brought them so close that before the graininess obliterated the details I could clearly identify the back-brace guy and see enough of the other men's faces to run an ID check on them if I had to. I lucked out on one photo that showed my guy bending over at the waist apparently tying his shoes. One of the security lights had caught his face at that very moment and he came out so clearly I could see the buttons on his shirt. So, in the end, technology saved the day after all.

Although I had been a fool not to have done it the day before, I called one of my NYPD friends and had him run a check on the Nissan registration. It turned out the owner had a criminal record more than a cubit long with convictions, jail time and parole for illegal gambling and racketeering. The vice squad had labeled him as a person of interest but hadn't had the manpower to do a thorough investigation of what he was currently up to. I was asked to email my photos to one of the detectives on the case with a brief explanation of the who-what-why-where-when and how.

It took several months for all of this to unravel itself but the cops were able, with the help of my pictures, to identify everyone who had met at the car dealership that night. They had never heard of the guy I had tailed but he turned out to be the one who turned evidence on the others in return for a short sentence and a long probation. The investigation showed they had been strong-arming legitimate car dealers to sell stolen vehicles with fake ID numbers. The IDs were cloned from real cars that had been sent to wrecking yards without having been reported to CarFax. If someone ran a check on the car's ID, it would look to be as clean as a three-game sweep of the Yankees. As a bonus, the buyers would have the added assurance they were buying the car from an authorized dealer.

As for my guy, he got nailed by both his former employer and the insurance company that had hired me. In a separate trial on the insurance fraud, he received almost exactly the same jail time he had saved by being a canary in the criminal case. So, in the end, justice was served.

The insurance company gave me a generous "thank you" that left me with enough left over to put it into a savings account. I have never been good about stashing money under the mattress for a rainy day but I opened up this account for Mona and me; planning for the day when we amalgamate our holdings and enter into a corporate merger "for as long as we both shall live."

Sunday morning I went to church with Mona, something I have been doing off and on since my first visit on Christmas Eve. The pastor was nice enough to let us use her office to change our clothes after the service. Since we were going to the opera that afternoon we figured we would go in style. I donned an old tuxedo I had worn back in the days when I had sung tenor in the university men's chorus. Mona had stopped by her folk's place in Jersey and dug out an old prom dress from high school. To her surprise it still fit; more or less. She had to split a few seams and close them up with a needle, some thread and a half dozen safety pins. I presented her with an old-fashioned Cattleya orchid corsage, which made her smile like a teenager getting her first kiss. She looked gorgeous to me although, to the people who saw us at the Met, we probably looked like refugees from a thrift shop. But we didn't care and with our noses in the air we took our seats in the nose-bleed section, fought back the feeling of vertigo and had ourselves a great time.

We drank champagne during intermission and I got bruised ribs from Mona who elbowed me every time I tried to sing along under my breath. Carmen died wonderfully and, at the end we joined everyone else by doing what a hen does when she lays an egg after rising from her nest. Mona added another bruise to my ribs when I told her that what the hen did was a standing ovation.

After I fell asleep that night, I dreamed I was standing at Castle Clinton in Battery Park with a giant, old-fashioned camera. Unlike the ruin it is today, the fort was completely intact and the view to the south was missing both the Verrazano Bridge and the Statue of Liberty. The river was filled with sailing ships of all kinds as though the idea of a steam engine hadn't yet registered in anyone's imagination. I tried to take a picture but every ship was moving around as fast as a speeding bullet. When I pulled out the glass plate from the camera it showed the river but without a ship in sight.

On Monday morning I planned to spend time researching the genealogy case. My client had explained that her family's oral history preserved the memory of a ship called the *Chimera* that sailed from South America and brought their family patriarch to New York in the year 1810. The assumption was that this ancestor had been either Spanish or Portuguese, and that upon his arrival in the United States he had changed his name from Reyes to King.

Nautical practice has been to record every significant ship that sails into or out of a major harbor. Why this is done, I have no idea but, like photographs, these records capture moments in time that can often be connected from one port of call to another like pearls on a necklace.

The thought of the *Chimera* brought back a hazy memory of my dream the night before. The thought of invisible sailing ships made me think of things like the

Bermuda Triangle and sailor's tales of phantom ships under full sail but without a single crew member on board. Maybe this *Chimera* was one of those phantom ships aimlessly wandering the seven seas with a skeleton crew seeking a safe harbor and never finding one.

It took me most of the day but eventually I tracked down the arrival of the *Chimera* into New York harbor on October 14, 1820. If it was the same ship that brought my client's family to America then the dates of their personal legend would have to be revised forward ten years. By a stroke of luck, 1820 was the first year the formal records of immigrants to New York began to be kept. There was no one named Reyes on the ship but there was a William King. Had he changed his name before arriving in America? Or was that his real name all along? And where did he board the ship? Good questions and I needed some answers.

I arranged to pay my mirror image in Buenos Aries to do the same thing there that I had been doing here. Only I gave him the arrival date of the ship in New York which made his job a lot easier. A trip from Argentina to New York would have taken fifteen weeks based on some research I had done. This would include time spent in ports of call collecting provisions and time spent on making minor repairs to the vessel along the way.

I have to give the guy credit. He took only two days to find that the ship's departure date had been listed as March 8, 1820, just as the winter season was ending in the southern hemisphere. The trouble with this date was to explain why it took thirty weeks to get from there to here. Like the ships in my dream, the *Chimera* had sailed over the horizon and become invisible for over seven months. To make it even more complicated, except for Rio de Janeiro there was not another harbor between Argentina and Florida that served as a routine port of call on the southern continent.

I sent a follow-up email to my man in Buenos Aires asking if he had seen any other information about the ship besides the departure date. He replied almost immediately.

"Yes," he wrote in the e-mail, "there was other information but I didn't think you would be interested. All you asked for was a departure date and that is what I gave you. I charged you for that but I'll give the other piece of information to you for free. The register said the *Chimera* was sailing under a British flag. I hope that helps. *Do svidaniya*, José."

The piece of information was helpful because it offered an alternative theory for the ship's itinerary. What if it had sailed from Argentina to England before heading to New York? In this scenario the ship would have likely crossed the Atlantic and sailed up the coast of West Africa possibly stopping off in the Azores or Canary Islands along the way.

I called my client, explained the situation and the cost of my investigation so far, and then asked how much more she was willing to spend on the matter. She said if I spent wisely and well she would be content knowing all that could have been done had been done.

So I made a contact with another mirror image of myself in London giving him a range of probable dates to help narrow the search. First off he found the *Chimera* on the list of ships registered in England and authorized to fly under the British flag. The ship was a packet with two square-rigged masts and room for 80-100 passengers. He added a few more pearls to the strand by finding the *Chimera* had docked in London on July 22 and discharged all of its cargo and many of its passengers. Several passengers came on board when it left London on August 15. Even more boarded when the ship made outgoing stops at Southampton and Liverpool before heading out across the Atlantic for its seven to eight-week voyage to New York.

In response to a question, he said, yes, he had found a record of a passenger named William King who had boarded the ship in Liverpool. How he located all this I have no idea. But I do know he charged me $500 for his trouble. My client said it was worth every penny. She didn't even sound disappointed to learn that her family origins were probably from Britain instead of Iberia or the pampas of Argentina. This was, in fact, an advantage because the family name had not been changed from one thing to another. As a bonus, because its origin appeared to be from one of the most genealogically researched nations on earth it would be easy for her to trace the family history back even further.

The case was a happy success so far as it went. I got paid and I managed to have my client pay two other people who did much of the work she was paying me to do. Sometimes I love what I do. This was one of those times.

Somehow, as it flowed from deep inside my subconscious, my dream about New York Harbor had brought together all the things that had been stirring in my mind the past few weeks. If I was to analyze the dream with a Freudian psychotherapist we would no doubt gain insight by associating the missing ships on the photographic plate with the disappearance of my mother when I was a child and the death of my father when I was eighteen. There would, of course, also be a sexual aspect to the dream with the ships sailing so quickly in and out and in and out of the narrow entrance to New York Harbor.

If it was Jung instead of Freud the dream would offer the universal phallic symbolism of ship's masts and the vast expanse of water representing not only life but the threat of chaos and danger as well. The arrival of the *Chimera* in New York on October 14 would also be important as that day in 1820 would have occurred under the sign of Libra which is, as everyone knows . . . .

This is all nonsense to me, of course. I don't have the insurance or the cash to pay for a therapist and I wouldn't go to one even if I had money to burn; at least not for a dream. If I was suffering from some mental or emotional condition that needed some serious attention then that might be a different story, but given that my life is a happy one, I am content to let my dream be simply a dream. A dream, however, that reminded me there is sometimes more to life than meets the eye; and that just because you can't see something doesn't prove that it doesn't exist. Like a soldier standing guard in Ford's Theater; like crooks meeting inside a car lot showroom; like a phantom ship coming from a direction you hadn't considered; or like lovers who have lived together for such a long time they have, for all practical purposes, become invisible to one another both at the dinner table and in bed.

My dream and everything that went with it made me wonder if I had fallen into the habit of moving around so quickly that I had become an invisible blur in Mona's emotional camera. Attending the opera had provided a good excuse for us to slow down and actually see one another once again.

It crossed my mind that if Mona and I were to become invisible to one another it would not be a dream, it would be a nightmare.

Without wasting another minute, I called her on the phone and asked if she wanted to go to a movie.

Chapter 12

Arson & Old lace
April

It was 10:30 a.m. on a Monday morning. I had just interviewed a woman who had been an eyewitness to a car accident. The drivers involved had accused each other of being at fault and the insurance company had hired me to see what I could find out. My conclusion, after completing the interview, was that both drivers should have their licenses revoked, their heads examined and their mouths washed out with soap.

The woman I interviewed told me she was standing on the corner of an empty intersection waiting for the pedestrian light to change. Since there were no cars in sight, she had considered jay walking but since she was in no hurry and the sunset was so beautiful, she decided she would just wait the extra fifteen seconds and go with the green. Just before she expected the light to change she heard the sound of a car speeding towards the intersection from her left and, at the same moment, saw a car speeding down the street in front of her. The car on the left appeared to be trying to beat the yellow light and the other car appeared to be trying to time the green light as closely as possible. Because of a building on the corner, neither driver could see the other.

The witness described how the car on her left hit the intersection a millisecond before the yellow light turned red and the car coming toward her hit the intersection a millisecond before the red light turned green. Or, she said, it might have been that the car on her left crossed into the intersection a millisecond *after* the yellow light had turned red and the other car crossed into the intersection a millisecond *after* the red light had turned green. Or, she said, the two lights might have been slightly out of sequence with the yellow light turning red milliseconds before the red light turned green or it might have been the other way around where the red light had turned green before the yellow light had turned red. "It all happened so quickly I just can't be sure."

The one thing she *was* clear about was that the pedestrian light turned green at the same moment the two cars collided in the center of the intersection—left front-end to right front-end—a collision that sent the cars sliding side by side across to the opposite corner, taking out a stoplight, a streetlight, a street sign, a mailbox, three newspaper stands and a fire hydrant.

If I was Solomon I'd say, "Just cut the baby in half and be done with it."

Based on what I heard about them, I figured the two drivers would be stupid enough to think that getting half a baby each would be a good deal.

200

As it turned out, this is exactly what I wrote down and turned in to the insurance company. Even the part about King Solomon. I didn't expect the insurance company to pay me anything for submitting a report like that but, to my surprise, I received a nice check attached to an equally nice letter thanking me for helping them settle the claim fairly and equitably.

What I didn't know then but know now is that both drivers were covered by the same insurance company. I am so glad the sign over my door says "Mike Maurison, Private Eye" instead of "Mike Maurison, Insurance Claims Adjuster."

As I sat down at my desk, the phone rang. It was Mona.

"Guess what!" she said in an excited, high-pitched voice. "Chia just phoned to say that she and Robert have set the date for their wedding. It's going to be next month on May 19th. Check your calendar and if you have any commitments or appointments on that day, cancel them! Oh, this going to be wonderful!"

Weddings are nice. It's nice to see happy people. Receptions are usually nice, too, but there is usually too much milling about for my taste. If I can get away with it, I usually grab a plate of food and find a quiet corner somewhere out of the way where I can sit until I've been there long enough to leave without looking like a boor. For Robert and Chia, though . . . and for Mona . . . I'll hang in there 'til the bitter end. After all, that's what friends are for.

But Mona was still talking.

"Chia was baptized Catholic and Robert doesn't have a church background and because they didn't want to wait for six months they couldn't get married in a Catholic Church so they found a Spanish speaking protestant church on the Upper West Side and made arrangements with the pastor to be married there. Chia's family is from Puerto Rico and most of them speak Spanish as their first language so that's why they chose a Spanish-speaking church. They've been going to pre-marriage counseling for the past two months and didn't even tell me about it! But I am so happy for them. I can't wait. Chia asked me to be her bridesmaid and said Robert would be giving you a call, too. She didn't say what he was going ask you, but . . . ."

I cut in and carried the thought along.

" . . . but you guess he's going to ask me to be one of his groomsmen, right?"

I told her that while she had been talking I had put a small heart on my calendar with the letters "R & C" in the middle of May 19. Mona said that was so cute and that she had to get back to work so "Bye."

I pondered the question whether Robert would make the effort to say, "I do" or whether he would keep in character by saying, "Sure." No doubt that would be, for me, the most eagerly anticipated moment in the ceremony.

The light on my answering machine was blinking. It was another message from my Aunt Lucille.

This time, instead of saying "Hello, I just wanted to let you know I have been thinking of you lately, etc.," she said, "Nesbitt . . . I mean, Mike. This is your Aunt Lucille. Please call me. I need to talk with you as soon as possible."

Once again, my finger hovered over the delete button but this time I couldn't bring myself to push it. Perhaps the time had come for me to reconnect with my family instead of avoiding them as I'd done for all these years. So, with my guts murmuring something that I assumed to be an encouraging word, I did the impossible. I picked up the phone and punched in the numbers for Aunt Lucille.

She answered the phone and before I could say "Hello" she said, "Oh, Mike. I am so glad you called me back so quickly."

I assumed she had caller ID on her phone but, as it turned out I was wrong. Somehow she just "knew" it was going to be me on the other end of the line.

"I thought you would want to know that your Uncle Al passed away last night. We thought he had caught the flu but it turned into pneumonia and before I could get him to a doctor, he stopped breathing. The EMTs did what they could but he didn't respond. Neither of us have much of a family left. For me it is only your two cousins and you. I just wanted you to know."

She paused as if waiting for me to say something. For the first time I thought of Aunt Lucille as a regular human being instead of a predatory ogre. Part of me felt humbled that after all these years of ignoring her she still wanted me to be a part of her life. The other part of me just felt bad for being such a self-centered cad. All this went through my emotional processor in about half a second.

The words "I am so sorry" came out of my mouth before I could even think of what to say.

The words were filled with emotion and seemed to come from somewhere deep down in my soul. Tears came to my eyes; tears I never dreamed I would shed for Aunt Lucille.

"How are Benny and Connie taking it?"

The words flowed as easily as wine from bottle.

"Ben's on his way from Albany and Connie lives just two miles away in Brentwood so she's been with me since last night. I'm doing all right but I don't think any of it has started to sink in yet. Oh, Mike, it is so good to be talking to you. I hope you can come over for a visit. I'm sure there will be a service or a funeral or something and I would like you to come to that, too."

Talking with Aunt Lucille was hard enough but driving over to Islip and sitting in her home talking about the people and things I had ignored or shut out of my life for twelve years did not appeal to me.

All I could bring myself to say was, "Yes, of course I'll come. Just let me know. I'm so glad you phoned to tell me about your . . . my . . . about Al. And like I said, I'm so sorry. I'll keep in touch. I promise."

Why I promised to "keep in touch" I'll never know. I guess I just got carried away with trying to say the right things. Guilt is hard to deal with sometimes, especially when you are forced to face up to it. I suppose I had a decision to make: A) I could let the guilt destroy me; B) I could try to shove it back where I had kept it buried all these years; or, C) Using a perfectly good biblical word, I could repent, let go of the guilt and start over as though the past twelve years hadn't happened. I have never done well on multiple-choice exams so I just went "I love you; I love you not" and chose answer "C." It was the right choice. I knew this guilt thing needed to be cut off and left somewhere to die. To do this I needed to reconnect with

Aunt Lucille and my cousins before any of *us* died. The thought of dying sobered me up from my morning cup of coffee.

I took out my calendar and put a small cross next to yesterday's date and below it I wrote the words, "Uncle Al."

I felt exhausted, as if I had put in a full-day's work. But when I checked my watch it only said 11:15 a.m. It wasn't even time for lunch yet.

There was a second message on the answering machine. I had gotten so worked up about Aunt Lucille that I hadn't even noticed it was there. It turned out to be another insurance claims case but with a different company. It seems there had been a storage room fire. The police said there was no evidence of arson but the insurance company wasn't convinced. The company offered to pay me to visit the site and to check out the claimant, the building owner, the facility manager and anything or anyone else I thought might be relevant. I'd done work for them before and had saved them so much money over the years they didn't feel any need to micromanage my investigation.

I took the case and, after a few questions, got the basic facts down on a piece of paper. The fire had broken out in a mini storage unit in Hell's Kitchen six days earlier at about 4:00 a.m. Rebecca McCrae, the woman renting the destroyed unit, claimed to have been storing large, archived collections of 18th-19th century French silhouettes and 17th-19th century European lace. The collections were insured for a total $850,000. The fire had gutted her unit, and the units adjacent to it were severely damaged, mostly by water. The police had decided the fire had been caused by a malfunctioning electrical outlet so they had dropped the case as fast as they had picked it up. Private investigators like me are not called in because we are better at this sort of thing than the police. We are, in fact, at a distinct disadvantage because we do not have the legal flexibility and laboratory resources that they do. On the other hand, we have time to look into things more thoroughly because we don't have to do triage to decide which cases to pursue and which cases to drop.

My afternoon was free so I grabbed a pre-packaged egg salad sandwich at Juan's corner market and caught the subway down and across town to Hell's Kitchen. The exterior of the four-story storage building showed no sign that there had been a fire. I had no authorization to enter, but after I explained who I was and what I was doing there, the manager said I could take a look at the mess.

"After all," she said, "it's not a crime scene and the renter cleared her stuff out, ended her lease and left it for me to clean up. That means I can show it off to whoever I want, right?"

I wasn't going to argue over something that was to my advantage so I kept my mouth shut and up we went to the fourth floor. The storage units were individually self-contained with sheet-metal walls, heavy-duty cyclone fencing for roofs and- roll-up doors. The units were about ten feet high inside but the fourth floor ceiling was a good fifteen feet higher than that. The large floor area held hardly any trace of smoke. But a damp, sooty smell grew stronger as we neared the area of the fire.

All of the affected units were empty and scrubbed clean except for McCrae's. Hers was still a wet, sloppy pile of mushed paper, charred cardboard and melted, plastic storage tubs. It looked as though it had been picked over and, if there had ever been anything worth salvaging it had been taken long before I got there.

When I was little my father would sometimes take me to Coney Island for an outing on Saturdays or Sundays. There was a man who called himself "The Wizard of Scissors." If you paid him and sat still for a few minutes, he would cut out the shape of your profile on a piece of black paper and attach it to a small piece of white poster-board. Years later I learned that when an image that is too dark to show details is set against a brightly lit background it is called a silhouette. As art, silhouettes are generally made with black and white paper. Head profiles, birds, trees, leaves, animals, landscapes and big-city skylines have all been popular subjects for silhouettes. As a recognized art, the silhouette had its heyday in Western Europe during the 17th, 18th and 19th centuries. There are so many of these old silhouettes around that Antique Road Show appraisers probably roll their eyes when they see one. Even so, there are some that are quite valuable. It wouldn't take much of a fire mixed with water from a sprinkler system or a fireman's hose to turn even a large collection of silhouettes into pulp in a matter of seconds. Like I said, there was lots of mushed paper on the cement floor but none of it came even close to being recognizable.

Lace is also a rather esoteric art form with a limited constituency of collectors. I won't go into the history of lace but if you are interested you can look it up on-line like I did with the silhouette info.

There were bits and pieces of what looked like charred lace scattered on the floor, mixed in with the charred and mushed paper. The lace brought back memories of my grandmother, who would often sit and knit things like sweaters or "afghan" comforters. At other times, she would make things out of lace; things I could never see much use for. My grandmother called it tatting and she used hooked needles to tie and re-tie linen thread into elaborate patterns. From what I have read antique lace can be very valuable; especially if a piece is connected to a historical person, place, or event.

Yet even if this had been one of the largest and finest collections of silhouettes and lace in the world I was having a hard time adding it up to $ 850,000 worth of paper and thread.

When I asked, the manager was kind enough to give me several self-sealing sandwich bags. I put some of the mushed paper in one and some bits of the charred lace in the others. Back in the corner was a burned out electrical outlet the police had determined to be the source of the fire. There were still a few puddles of water left. In the reflected light I could see a thin sheen of something on the surface of the water. Not knowing what else to do I touched the surface of one of the plastic baggies against the water in the hopes that whatever it was would adhere to it. Then that baggie went into another baggie. As I turned around to leave I felt something semi-solid go squish under my shoe. It turned out to be a small piece of wax, flattened by my foot. After looking around I found another piece in the same area as the first . . . right next to the burned electrical outlet. The wax went into another baggie.

I didn't have time to set up any interviews that afternoon but I did have time to check out some personal information concerning what the insurance company would call, "people of interest."

It turned out the owner of the building was going through bankruptcy with the State of New York as a result of putting all of his eggs into a scheme to make electricity from the bobbing of twenty-five thousand large buoys off the coast of Nova Scotia. A lien had been placed on all his holdings including the storage building. For the life of me, I couldn't see how burning up a fourth-floor storage unit would have been of any benefit to either him or his creditors. The manager, who I had met, would have had nothing to gain from a fire like that either. I suppose she could have lost her job and been blessed by the opportunity to collect unemployment insurance but the advantages seemed to be more than offset by the probability of receiving a felony conviction for arson.

As far as I could tell, there were only two reasonable explanations: First, the fire was caused by a faulty electrical outlet or, second, it was intentionally started by Ms. McCrae. After all, whatever valuables she had in that storage unit were, and I don't mean this to sound like a pun, probably more valuable on paper than at an art auction . . . not to mention they were most certainly more valuable for their insured value than for what they were actually worth. I handed the baggies over to a privately-operated forensics lab on the Upper West Side being very specific as to the tests I wanted them to conduct.

The next day I did some research on Rebecca McCrae. It seems that after the fire, she had cleared out of New York City as fast as she could, leaving only a post office box address in Phoenix as a point of contact. The insurance company had a cell phone number and an email address for her. Both were still active but no one was answering. Her last communication with the insurance company was to tell them that from then on she would be speaking to them only through her attorney. The chances of me getting an appointment to interview her seemed slimmer than a hair's breadth on a razor hog.

To their credit the NYPD had noted in their report that she had signed into her storage unit for a visit three days before the fire. The security video showed her busy hauling things back and forth from her rental car until she signed out and left at 4:27 p.m., about sixty hours before the fire alarm went off. No one had entered her unit or any of the adjacent units after she had left. When questioned by the police she provided the names of two witnesses who vouched for her being in Queens from that evening until early afternoon on the day of the fire. It was an airtight alibi and, in the absence of a timed incendiary device the police had been inclined to remove her as a suspect.

I phoned in a preliminary report to the insurance company and went back to my apartment to do more research on silhouettes, antique lace and Ms. McCrae on the internet. It turned out there were plenty of Rebecca McCraes in various places around the world but none of them bore any resemblance to the one who had shown up in New York City to file an insurance claim for $850,000 in a storage unit fire and then vaporized into thin air. I was still mulling over why anyone in their right mind would store anything worth that much in a mini-storage facility. Nothing made sense and nothing added up which was, of course, the reason the insurance company had hired me in the first place.

True to their word the forensic lab had their analysis completed in less than forty-eight hours. None of the results surprised me. The three tests I was most interested in came back as follows: The shiny stuff floating on top of the water was paraffin. The wax I had stepped on was a highly compact mixture of beeswax and soy. Some, but not all of the lace scraps had been made with rayon or polyester thread.

Depending on who and what a person's interests are, these results could well lead two people to come to different conclusions. Personally, I'm working on the assumption that Rebecca McCrae started the fire to get the insurance money.

In my scenario, McCrae had a few authentic silhouettes and some genuine antique lace. Whatever else she had was phony, fake or forged, take your pick. She then either tricked or paid off an appraiser to make up an inventory list of the imagined items, giving them a value that would be high-end in the collectors market. She used this list to take out an insurance policy and then arrived in New York where she placed everything in a mini-storage unit. After what seemed to be a reasonable amount of time, she removed whatever there was that had any value and replaced it with more worthless imitations.

She knew that in a fire virtually everything made of paper would be reduced to ashes or charred pulp. Any scraps of lace left behind would provide evidence her imagined collections had, indeed, been destroyed. To be on the safe side she probably burned the stuff and turned

211

it into pulp before she even put in back into storage. After holding test-runs in her apartment and getting the timing down she set up a long-burning candle in the back corner of the storage unit next to an electrical outlet that would later appear to be the source of the fire. On-line retailers sell candles that will burn for over 100 hours and cook you breakfast as a bonus. Some well-designed home-made candles smaller than a gallon milk container can burn for up to four weeks. Beeswax/soy is a common blend in such long-burning candles. A small candle burning for sixty hours would not be a difficult thing to set up. The small flame and lack of any significant smoke or heat would pose no risk of setting off a fire or smoke alarm.

Knowing that flammable fuels would be easily identifiable after the fire she only used highly combustible material that would be quickly and completely consumed, leaving no trace. My guess was she used piles of crumpled wax paper as her starter fuel. The only trace remaining from them was the thin sheen of paraffin floating on the top of the water puddles.

Since polyester and rayon are both early 20th century inventions their presence in lace supposedly created in the 17th-19th centuries would be impossible. If the insurance company wanted to spend more money, the scraps of lace that had been made from linen or cotton thread could be tested for carbon 14 to determine what century the fiber was grown. My guess is they would also prove to be 20th century.

Like I said, this is only one way to explain the evidence. I have no doubt McCrae's attorneys will find their own ways to twist it into different shapes. In the end, though, it will be up to a jury to decide which, if any, explanation makes sense "beyond a reasonable doubt."

Poor old Becky might have pulled the whole fraud off except for three things. First, she insured the stuff for too much. This raised red flags and drew more scrutiny to her claim than was necessary. Second, there were the two pieces of wax that got my mind spinning a scenario made out of gossamer. And third, there was the wax paper that came back from the dead, rising to life again as paraffin floating on the surface of a puddle left behind by a fire hose.

I had finished with my small part in the investigation so I turned my findings over to the insurance company for their lawyers to sort out. I was well paid for my trouble and the whole thing took only five days. Five days during which I had completely forgotten about Aunt Lucille.

The whole thing about her and Uncle Al came back to me on my way home from hand-delivering the signed and notarized copy of my report to the insurance company's main office in Lower Manhattan. As soon as I walked into my apartment I picked up the phone and called her.

"Aunt Lucille?"I began. "I'm sorry to have been out of the loop this past week. Please, can you bring me up to date?"

She was, of course, glad to hear from me. She was feeling more devastated than she had thought possible but was sure that with the support of her two children— and me—she would be all right soon enough. The memorial service for Al had been scheduled three weeks from now on May 18th.

I told her what I had told her before, "Don't worry, I'll be there. I promise."

If I had bothered to double-check my calendar, I would have noticed a small heart sketched in for the day afterwards. It wasn't until days later I considered the possibility there might be a wedding rehearsal on the 18th. My rule of thumb has become: "Even when things seem to be going my way they sometimes wind up missing me by a mile."

Later that evening my phone rang. It was Robert.

"What's up, dude?" I said giving my best Southern California surfer impression.

It wasn't a very good impression but Robert had the good grace to ignore it and get down to business.

"Mike, I want to ask if you'll be a part of my wedding."

"Of course I will," I said. "I'll do whatever needs to be done. I'll do the guest book, pass out favors, take pictures . . . what the hey . . . I'll even cut the cake for you if you don't want to do it yourself!"

"No," Robert said in his usual stoic manner. "I think Chia has all of that covered already. And don't even think about cutting our cake because I will be the guy holding the knife, *capische*?"

And here I had thought Robert was Scottish. Now he's Italian.

"Mike, listen to me. I want you to be my Best Man. I want you to be the friend who stands next to me when I get married and I want you to be the friend who offers us the first toast at our reception."

I was stunned. I had no idea Robert considered me to be that close of a friend. I had treated him like a jerk more than once and now . . . .

"Mike?" it was Robert again. "Are you still there?"

"Yes, Robert," I said. "I'm still here. And I would like to be the Best Man at your wedding."

There was a pause and then Robert asked, "How do you mean that? Do you mean "I would like to, 'But?'" or "I would like to, 'Yes?'"

"*Yes*," I said with as much emphasis on the "Yes" that I could put on it. "But why are you asking me? I'm honored to be asked but I didn't know I was . . . well . . . no, don't answer. You don't have to answer. It's okay. You asked, I'm honored, I said 'Yes' and we're both happy. Thanks for asking. Mona and I are both really looking forward to the wedding. And now we both get to be a part of it. Who woulda figured."

"Mike," Robert continued. "I'm asking you because you were one of the first people since I was in high school who actually noticed that I existed—not counting my parents and my friends at the curling club. You have no idea how much I looked forward to you stopping by at the museum. You sometimes made me feel as though the only reason you came was to say "Hi" to me. I want to thank you for that."

This was news to me. I had always felt our relationship had, in some unfathomable way; grown into a friendship of some sort and I always liked it when Robert called me Mr. Maurison at the entrance door to the MoMA. To tell the truth, I even liked it when we went out a couple times for a beer after the museum closed. But the rest of it? I had no idea Robert felt this way about

215

me. Sometimes we can be so focused on ourselves htat we forget to notice the effect we are having on the people around us. This time I must have gotten lucky. Without knowing it I had done something good instead of just being my natural, socially inept self.

Robert kept on talking. "The other reason I'm asking you is because of Chia. We never would have met if it hadn't been for you."

Again, I was surprised. But this time I asked him what he meant.

"You remember the day I met Chia at Coney Island?"

"Of course I do," I replied. "That was the same day I met Mona."

"When you came up and sat down next me on the bench, I was sitting, staring out at the water with my back to the Boardwalk. Do you remember that?"

"Yeah, you were eating a pretzel."

"And after we'd been there a while you asked if I wanted to take a walk on the Boardwalk towards Brighton. You could have chosen to go the other direction or you could have just said, 'Nice seein' you Robert. Have a nice day," or you could have just sat there with me for a few more minutes nursing your beer. But you didn't. You said let's go this way. So I stood up, turned around, took a few steps and there was Chia. Without you it would never have happened. So . . . that's the other reason I'm asking you to be the Best Man at my wedding. It's the only way I can think of to say, 'Thank you.'"

I didn't know what to say. So I pretended I was Robert and just nodded my head.

Chapter 13

New Beginnings
May

Even if "April showers bring May flowers" isn't really a joke about the Pilgrims it can still be sort of funny. For me the "April showers" were wedding ones for Chia and the "May flowers" are the ones she'll be carrying down the aisle on the 19th when she becomes Mrs. Robert Frasier.

I say this is funny because, just a year ago, imagining Robert getting married to anybody would have been like imagining Ron Howard as a model for a shampoo commercial. Robert does have the hair, but to put it nicely he lacks the sort of *savoir faire* that once drew women to people like Clark Gable in *Gone With the Wind*.

When I first met Robert guarding the front entrance to the Museum of Modern Art he would nod and sometimes say "Good afternoon." After a while he started to put more words together in a row by saying things like, "Good morning, Mr. Maurison." Once in a while, on special occasions, he would even find the courage to express himself in a full sentence or a short paragraph. Since he met Chia seven months ago a previously-hidden inner Robert has emerged—a Robert who sometimes talks as though he was in the process of reinventing the run-on sentence. It has been like watching Robert morph from being silent Cal Coolidge into being Jack Kerouac, pouring an infinite stream of consciousness onto an infinite roll of paper with an infinite supply of verbal ink.

A month ago, I worried if the old Robert might say "Sure" instead of "I do" at the wedding. Now I worry the pastor won't be able to get a word in edgewise. As Robert's Best Man, I am hoping the old Robert will show up, at least for the ceremony. After it's all over I don't mind if the new and improved Robert comes to the reception or goes on the honeymoon. That's because at the reception I'll be able to sit down and, on the honeymoon, it will be Chia who'll have to deal with it.

What I've had to deal with lately has been trying to come up with creative ideas for excusing myself from co-ed wedding showers. Although Robert would welcome my company, he understands me well enough to know I would rather crawl through barbed wire than sit around all afternoon sipping tea and nibbling *petit fours, canapés* and those little triangular sandwiches with the crusts cut off.

What I prefer to do is sleuth.

Sleuthing means sneaking around. It is a synonym for being a snoop which is, of course, someone who sticks their nose into other people's business; preferably without their knowing. Maybe that is not exactly right. It would be more accurate to say that what I prefer to do is to get *paid* for being a sleuth. If the one thing doesn't lead to the other then it is just a hobby I can't afford. Fortunately there always seems to be someone who is willing to pay me to crouch behind a garbage can all night or to drive some complicated route through Manhattan, Brooklyn and Queens at different times of the day and week using a stopwatch to compare the times. Sometimes it can be very boring—but not always.

Take last Friday night, for example. Mona wanted her family to meet Robert and Chia so she invited Robert and Chia, along with her sister-in-law, Pam, her nephew Danny, her parents and me to her apartment for dinner. Even though her two roommates had politely made other plans for the evening we still found ourselves sitting on each other's laps in the small living room area. Afterwards, while the women ate dessert and talked about whatever it is that women are interested in talking about, the four men planned to catch some fresh air by walking over to "The Golden Pool" for some billiards. Only three of the men ever got there, though, because as we were walking out of Mona's apartment building my phone rang.

It was Drew Martini, a man who had recently hired me to investigate two sets of tenants who were renting units in a townhouse he owned in Soho. If he wasn't living in Baltimore he probably would have been doing the investigation on his own time but that is where he was so I had been put on his time card.

"Maurison," he said when I answered the phone. "Are you free?"

"No," I said without missing a beat. "You know I'm not free. I charge by the hour. And, by the way, who is this?"

Drew had his caller ID blocked so he always showed up as "Unknown Caller." He sounded impatient and a little irritated.

"This is Drew, the man who is paying you to work for him. Do you want the job or should I call someone else who is hungrier?"

"You called the right guy, Drew. What's up?"

"You have the key with you? My manager phoned and said that it's happening there again right now. This is your chance to see it for yourself and, hopefully, to get me some answers. It might not happen again for who knows how long so the fire is hot and, like our contract puts it, you agree to be ready and willing to strike at a moment's notice. Well now's the moment and here's your notice. I don't care what you're doing right now. What I want is for you to gird up your loins and get over there before I'm through talking, got it?"

Drew is a very flexible guy, giving me lots of options.

So, of course, I chose Option #1 and said, "I'll be there in less than an hour."

That ended my male bonding experience for the evening. So I left my friends to beat their drums in the cave without me and scurried off to catch the #6 down to Spring Street.

After walking five blocks, I came to the address where Drew owned some townhouse units. They were called townhouse units to make them seem more upscale than they actually were. They were really just one- and two-bedroom, one bathroom apartments. But Soho has become up-scale enough for a man like Drew to make some real money as a landlord. So, of course, he is going to make his properties look and sound as trendy as possible. Not too far away is a five-story townhouse renting for $100,000 a month. Unlike Drew's units, it comes with its own swimming pool. But that wasn't my concern.

Drew's concern was that he suspected his tenants were subletting his apartments to other people in violation of their lease agreement. Subletting is a good way to make some money without having to tie up any of your own. Say you are renting a two-bedroom place for $3,000/month. You find someone who is desperate to hole up for some reason. You sublet one of the bedrooms for two thousand and you get a better deal than if you had split the rent with a roommate. As a bonus, the income is tax-free unless, like a good citizen, you take the high road and report it on your 1040.

The main problem with subletting is, of course, that both the owner and the sub-letters are getting ripped off. The reasons why sub-letters might be willing to get ripped off in exchange for a room are usually related to other problems. For example, they may in the country illegally; or they have zero credit; or they are trying to avoid being handed a warrant for their arrest. Folks like this are not usually considered as prime candidates for renting apartments in Lower Manhattan. Even so, because there are people like that all over the place, it isn't hard to see why unauthorized subletting is big business in the Big Apple.

From the sidewalk below I not only saw the silhouettes of people moving around in a third floor window but I also experienced the irony of standing a few blocks from Chinatown while listening to the sound of a mariachi band blaring down on me from the third floor.

New York is, of course, the original melting pot and I have always found the City's endemic cultural diversity to be one of its many charms. But what interested me at the moment was that the people who had leased Drew's units were named Kwon Lee and Izumi Tsuchida. Although cultural crossovers are more often the rule than the exception these days, I was betting that Kwon and Izumi had not been the ones who had hired the mariachi band.

Using the key Drew had given me I let myself into the building and took the elevator to the third floor. Drew's two-bedroom unit, which had been leased by Kwon, was as quiet as a church mouse. But the one-bedroom unit rented by Izumi sounded as lively as a margarita on steroids. I took a wild guess and concluded the unit was too small to hold both a party and a mariachi band at the same time but the stereo system had been good enough to fool me.

Every once in a while I could hear someone shouting *"Feliz cumpleaños"* or *"Salud."* I wished I had Chia with me but I knew enough to recognize the word *"salud"* as being a toast to someone's good health. I knew *"feliz"* meant "good" or "merry" or "happy" from hearing Jose Feliciano's *"Feliz Navidad"* thirty million times every Christmas on the radio and the *"años"* part meant year. Since it wasn't Christmas and it wasn't New Year's I figured I was standing a door's-width away from a blow-out birthday party.

I knocked on the door and a middle-aged man wearing a paper crown answered the door. Behind him were at least twenty people apparently having themselves very good time. The man looked at me curiously, as though he was trying to figure out who I was and why I was standing there.

"*¿Qué quiere?*" "What do you want?"

"I'm looking for Kwon Lee. Is he here?"

"I don't know Kwon Lee."

"How about Izumi Tsuchida? Is he here?"

"No. But he might be next door. You've got the wrong place."

And he closed the door.

I walked the ten steps back to the two-bedroom unit and knocked on the door. There was no answer. After a few more attempts to get someone's attention I took out Drew's key and let myself in. There was a bed in each bedroom, two desktop computers and a lot of clothing thrown around on the floor. A pile of beer bottles in a wastebasket and the sweet smell of new-mown hay complimented the apartment's aura of *fen shui*. After a quick phone conversation with Drew, I found a piece of paper, pulled out my pen and jotted down a short note:

Dear Mr. Lee and/or Mr. Tsuchida,

I am an agent for your landlord, Mr. Andrew Martini. He has asked me to tell you that he is not pleased with having your friends occupy his one-bedroom unit next door. I have assured him that they will be moving on to greener pastures by Sunday afternoon. After I determine how much your friends have been paying you for Mr. Martini's apartment, you will find that a surcharge of an equal or greater amount will be added to Mr. Tsuchida's monthly rent effective this coming Monday. Since the original lease agreement has been violated Mr. Martini is free to charge anything he wants until Mr. Tsuchida negotiates a new one or, after paying what is owed, moves out. If Mr. Martini does not hear from Mr. Tsuchida by Sunday evening he will initiate both a criminal complaint and an eviction notice the following morning.

Have a nice day.

Mike Maurison
Private Investigator

I left my business card attached to the note, let myself out and got back to Mona's place just twenty minutes after everyone else had left. Fortunately, she had a few *canapés* left for me to snack on while we filled each other in on our evening's adventures. We both agreed that except for me missing a chance to show the guys how to rip the felt while attempting a *massé* the night had been an unqualified success.

I should mention that Mona has forgiven my Aunt Lucille for scheduling my Uncle Al's memorial service the day before Robert and Chia's wedding. Mona says we'll just have to make the best out of what the Lord has given us to work with. After talking with Aunt Lucille, we were able to have the memorial service in Islip scheduled for 10:00 a.m. That will give us time to eat lunch as a family before heading back to Manhattan for the 5:00 p.m. wedding rehearsal.

I had everything under control until May 15th when it dawned on me my uncle's memorial service was just three days away. My guts started to rumble like Old Faithful does just before she erupts and I couldn't decide whether I needed an Alka-Seltzer, a quick trip to the men's room or a three-week "get-away-from-it-all" cruise in the South Pacific. I'm not usually a stressed-out kind of guy but the thought of meeting, eating and talking with Aunt Lucille, my cousins and their friends, was steering me towards a nervous breakdown.

I had hated, feared and despised Aunt Lucille ever since my mother left solely because of what my father had told me. Since that day, I had done everything I could to ignore her, even though she had done her best to be as loving and supportive as she could. Now I would have to face the consequences of my intransigence.

Until meeting Mona, I had never felt important enough to imagine myself in one of life's leading roles. I suppose that's why, when I first heard the story of the Prodigal Son, I felt I had more in common with the fatted calf than with any of the other characters. Now, all of a sudden, I felt like the youngest son, coming home covered in shame with my head down and my tail between my legs. In three days, I would be walking onto center stage with the spot light highlighting my every flaw. And even though I would be performing in a tragedy I honestly believed that my entrance would be greeted with laughter.

In my business, there are times when "fright and flight" is the best option. But this trip to Islip was not one of those times. Sooner or later, I needed to face the music and join my voice to the family choir. The whole thing was so new and intimidating that clichés and mixed metaphors were the only way I could find to describe my feelings.

Mona was very helpful and encouraging. From the beginning, she had made it clear she would go to the memorial service with me. She said it would be like going on a voyage of discovery like Magellan's where everything would be new and exciting. I reminded her that Magellan was killed in the Philippines and never made it back to Portugal. She then switched to using Captain Cook as an example but that didn't turn out to be very helpful either and for the same reason. I was beginning to feel like the character in Li'l Abner who had the storm cloud follow him around all the time. My life was like a ticking time bomb. I was doomed.

But Mona just kept laughing at me. Even though I never thought the situation was funny, her attitude did manage to put a more positive spin on it. When May 18th came along I felt like a kid standing on a diving board for the very first time, trying to work up the courage to jump off. Having once been that kid I could clearly remember the terror that moment held for me. Then again, I could also remember the thrill of leaping into thin air, the shock of hitting cold water and the pleasant surprise of discovering I didn't actually sink to the bottom of the pool like a rock. I had actually climbed out of the pool and jumped off the board a second time and then a third and a fourth. Maybe my day with Aunt Lucille would turn out to be like that. So, with Mona holding my hand, the two of us, like Butch Cassidy and the Sundance Kid, took the plunge together.

Because Uncle Al and Aunt Lucille had never been much for church, the memorial service took place at the local mortuary with a pastor called in from outside like a ringer on a softball team. To his credit, he had taken the time to meet with Aunt Lucille and talk with her about what the service would be like and what he might say that would make it more personal and meaningful for the family. Mona and I borrowed Sid's car and arrived thirty minutes early. We parked and walked in the front door. Aunt Lucille zeroed in on us like a cruise missile but instead of exploding, she wrapped her arms around me in a hug that would have knocked the air out of the lungs of an NFL lineman. If I had weighed thirty pound less, I believe she would have lifted me completely off of the floor.

I had not seen Aunt Lucile since my father's funeral. I had not talked with her then, nor had I talked with her since, until the phone conversation when she told me about Uncle Al's passing. Now, however, the conversation was face-to-face and there was no way I could hang up the phone.

"My, you look just like my sister," she said. "She was not the wisest woman in the world but she was a good woman in her own way."

I was struck by the way she spoke of my mother in the past tense. No one had heard a word from her since the day she left, so I had subconsciously placed her existence in a sort of limbo; a shadowy place where life and death merged into a reality custom-designed for my mother.

"I'll take that as a compliment," is all I could think to say. "It's good to see you again," I lied. "This is my friend, Mona."

Mona smiled that beautiful smile of hers and, to my surprise, it did not look at all forced. She actually seemed happy to meet my Aunt.

"A pleasure," she said, oozing with genuine sincerity. "Mike hasn't told me a lot about his family so I've been looking forward to meeting you all in person."

Aunt Lucille said much the same and then came the introductions to her daughter, Connie and her son, Ben. Connie was still single but Ben introduced his wife, Mindy, and their two toddler children, Sam and Susan. Neither cousin offered a hug but their handshakes were firm and polite, if not welcoming.

The pastor joined us and took us aside for a short prayer before we entered the chapel. During the prayer he said some of the same things I had heard Mona's pastor sayon the few Sundays I had gone to church with her. He spoke of "new life" and "resurrection" and, of course, "Jesus Christ." After he ended the prayer with an "Amen" we walked into the chapel like penguins on parade and sat down in the front chairs.

There were, perhaps, thirty or forty other people present without another child in sight. Most of the men looked as if they hadn't worn a tie for a long time. I figured they were either married to friends of Aunt Lucille or had been co-workers with Al at the Islip Water Department. Al had only been sixty years old but he had taken early retirement and had been off the job for nearly five years.

The service began with some quotes from the Bible and a prayer. Then the pastor read a sort of obituary about Al's life. He asked if anyone wanted to add a thought or share a memory about Al but no one raised

228

their hand or stood up to say anything. He then read another scripture about Jesus being the "resurrection and the life" and said some things about Jesus rising from the dead and showing us that life is stronger than death. I got the feeling it must have been a lot like the sermon I missed when I didn't go to the Easter service with Mona.

I'm not sure I got any comfort from the pastor's message but it did bring back some memories of the Christmas Eve service I'd attended with Mona. I recalled the feeling I had that night that maybe there was more to life than just the things we see and touch. This all means a lot to Mona and she keeps telling me it is part of who she is. If that's true, then I guess it's part of what I like about her, but I don't think about it very much except maybe at church or at funerals.

After the pastor closed out the service with the old cliché about "ashes and ashes, dust to dust" we walked down the street to a steak house and had a buffet lunch in the back room. Aunt Lucille kept busy talking with all the people who had come to pay their respects, and Benny and Connie spent most of the time talking to each other. After a while, Mona and I nodded that it was time to leave. We interrupted Aunt Lucille in the middle of a sentence, gave her a hug, said we'd had a good time under the circumstances, promised we would keep in touch, said, "Good-bye," and left.

As we walked back to the car I told Mona it hadn't been half as bad as I thought it would be. Mona laughed and said I had survived intact enough to return home which was more than could be said for Magellan or Cook. It had been an adventure, but not like jumping off a diving board where you want to climb out of the water and do it again.

Traffic was light on our way back to Manhattan. We put Sid's car back where it belonged and splurged on a cab for the half-mile ride to Mona's place. Since it wasn't even 2:30 p.m. yet and Mona's roommates were both at work, I sat down and watched some baseball on TV while Mona primped up for the wedding rehearsal. Mona changed into something new and I just wore what I had worn to the memorial service except for taking off the tie. New York being what it is we planned on taking an hour to get across town in a cab. New York being what it is we got to the church in fifteen minutes and had forty-five minutes to kill before the rehearsal started.

Fortunately, Robert arrived early, too. He looked confused and a little nervous but when he saw Mona and me, he relaxed and broke out into a sort of goofy smile. He asked about Uncle Al's service and how it went and I said I had felt like a piece of salmon mistakenly packed into a tin of sardines.

Chia arrived with her family. We met her parents, her brother Miggy, and her sister, Rita, who was also her Maid of Honor. Robert's family arrived soon after along with his groomsman, James, who was a friend from his curling team.

At 5:00 p.m., the minster arrived and explained we were going to learn the choreography so we wouldn't have to worry about it the next morning. That way we would all be able to enjoy the service without wondering where we were supposed to be standing. He also told stories about weddings where the groom had put his own wedding ring on the bride by mistake and the time when, after lighting

230

a unity candle, the bride and groom blew out each other's candles but the groom got carried away and blew melted wax all over the bride's face. She then spent the rest of the ceremony picking wax off of her face while trying hard not to laugh out loud. I suppose he told these stories to help calm everyone's nerves. Robert told me later that all it did was make him worry about what sort of disaster would make their wedding memorable enough for the pastor to talk about it at his next wedding rehearsal.

For me, at least, the rehearsal turned out well because I didn't trip over my feet escorting Rita down the aisle. The rehearsal dinner was down the street at a Mexican Cantina and, after eating too much and talking about nothing in particular, we all went home to rest up for the next day.

The wedding was scheduled to begin at 1:00 p.m. I thought that was an odd time to hold a wedding because it didn't give anyone enough time to eat lunch. At the rehearsal, the pastor told Robert to be sure and eat something before the service or he might pass out like another groom did at a wedding he had done. That anecdote worried Robert to the point that he ate two Big Mac extra value meals before leaving for the church.

I figured I would get up, shower and shave, put on my tuxedo, catch a cab to Mona's and off we would go to the wedding. I had forgotten that weddings were a big deal with the ladies.

Mona had scheduled a hair appointment at 8:00 a.m. After getting back to her apartment at 9:30, it took ninety minutes for her and her two roommates to get her makeup, necklace and earrings just right. When I stopped by to pick her up at 11 o'clock I was rested and as cool as a cucumber-bund. But Mona was already so exhausted that she would have fallen asleep in a second if lying down wouldn't have messed up her hair.

We sat in the back seat of the taxi with her bridesmaids dress draped across our laps. At the church she disappeared into the church nursery which had been designated the "Bridal Room" for the occasion. There, amidst the cribs and toys, Mona, Chia and Rita were primped and primed for battle by Chia's mother. Robert's mother stopped by to see if she could be of any help as did Mona's two roommates when they arrived. Robert spent the time sitting by himself in the pastor's study while James and I ushered people into the church. I had trouble remembering which side was the groom's side and which was the bride's side until James pointed out that where we would be standing during the wedding was the groom's side. At 1:10 p.m. I walked Robert's mother down the aisle with his father trailing behind and then James did the same with Chia's mother.

A friend of Chia's started playing guitar and singing a rather intense song called *Lucha de Gigante* while James and I joined Robert in the study. Robert handed me Chia's wedding ring, the pastor came in, had a short prayer and then led us into the church. When the song ended, the organist started playing Pachelbel's *Canon in D* while Mona and Rita walked slowly down the aisle to the front. I was amazed at how beautiful Mona looked in the pink and blue dress Chia had picked out. If she hadn't already been my girlfriend she would still have been the one I would have fantasized about in my dreams.

I was so busy looking at Mona that I never noticed Rita at all. I might have spent the rest of the ceremony staring at Mona except for the music suddenly switching to "Here Comes the Bride." Along with the first chord, Chia appeared arm-in-arm with her father. At that moment, Chia would have seriously challenged Mona as being the most stunningly beautiful woman in the room. I took a quick look at Robert. His eyes were as big as John Lennon's glasses and his mouth was twitching as if trying to decide what shape it should take.

It didn't take long for Chia to get to the front. Her father handed her over to Robert and gave him a very firm handshake and a smile that seemed out of place considering the killer look he shot at him. It was as if he was trying to say, "This is my daughter. If you ever do anything to hurt her I swear I will run you down with a steam roller."

After the drama of that moment the rest of the ceremony went along just like at the rehearsal. I lost my bet with Mona when Robert said, "I do" instead of "Sure" and I fulfilled my only responsibility by fishing Chia's ring out of my pocket. At the end of the ceremony the pastor pronounced them "husband and wife," Robert kissed the Bride, the pastor introduced them as Mr. and Mrs. Robert Frasier, we all walked down the aisle and the show was over. Looking back, I honestly can't remember anything happening that was strange enough for the pastor to share at his next wedding rehearsal.

There were only eighty or so people at the wedding, including Robert's family, members of his curling club and a few representative staff from the Museum. Chia's family was joined by some of her friends from high school and the whole crew from the beauty parlor. To my eternal gratitude they did not have a reception line so, after a few photos of Chia and Robert with and without family and attendants, we were all able to head straight down to the church's Fellowship Hall for the reception

I started the whole thing off with a toast I had carefully written out so I wouldn't sound like Robert Goulet trying to sing the American National Anthem:

"As Best Man I would like to propose a toast to Chia and Robert who are now married and stuck with each other for as long as they both shall live. Robert, may you hold and care for Chia with the same love and grace you hold and care for your curling stone. Chia, may you have the patience to teach Robert how to dance so you will move in harmony to the music that will flow from your lives together. May the two of you take the time to smile at each other at least once each day and may the sounds of Manhattan always remind you of the ever-present love and support of your family and friends. To Robert and Chia Frasier: *Salud!*

Everyone in the room said, *"Salud!"* and after that, the reception had nowhere to go but up.

True to his word and in a mock-threatening way, Robert waved the knife at me before he and Chia cut the cake. Robert's friend James caught the garter and, to my bemusement, Mona caught the bouquet. Because it was in a church, there was no alcohol and because there wasn't a lot of room in the hall there wasn't a dance floor either. But Chia's friend played a few songs on his guitar so Robert and Chia could dance with each other and with their parents.

Although we weren't part of the review, Mona and I stood off to the side and danced a few steps ourselves. It was the first time we had been that close for over a week.

The busy-ness of life sometimes seems to take the life out of too many people's lives so I made a mental note to never let that happen to Mona and me.

As we danced, it occurred to me that at that moment, the only cases left for me to solve were the mystery of life and death, the riddle of family and friends and the strange idea that two people can somehow become one. I wasn't sure I could come up with the solutions on my own but if Mona and I worked on them as a team, I figured we might be able to do the impossible.

As we finished our dance, I thought I saw Mona wiggle the ring finger on her left hand just a little. It might have been my imagination and I might have been mistaken but whether she wiggled it or not, the thought crossed my mind that now was as good a time as any.

So I got down on one knee, took her ring finger and held it in the way I would have held it if I had been holding a ring. I looked her in the eye and said, "Well?"

There was a short pause; a moment when the world slowed down and came to a stop. Then, with a smile that lit up the room like a flare, Mona leaned over, planted a sloppy kiss on my ear and whispered the word, "Sure."

BOOKS IN THE MIKE MAURISON SERIES

Book 1
I Want My MoMA
A Year in the Life of Mike Maurison, Private Eye

Book 2
To Have and To Hold
A Month in the Life of Mike Maurison, Private Eye

Book 3
Treasure Hunt
A Week in the Life of Mike Maurison, Private Eye

Book 4
Smoke and Mirrors
A Day in the Life of Mike Maurison, Private Eye

OTHER BOOKS BY JAMES A. TWEEDIE

Long Beach Short Stories

The One Who Tells the Stories

All books are published by Dunecrest Press and are
available on Amazon.com as paperback or Kindle

Made in the
USA
Middletown, DE